They were getting closer to the graveyard now, and they moved more and more cautiously, not willing to risk even another whisper. With the night as black as pitch, Steve did not expect to see a thing, but when he and Linda dropped to their knees and crawled between the wall and the lilacs, he was beginning to count on hearing plenty . . .

Then, in the silence, a stone rolled noisily and crashed to the ground. Linda sprang to her feet in horror. Two men were pounding for the wall, the torch they carried whipping a beam of light across Steve's face. Linda heard Robert's snarl of triumph as he ran. Steve's arm, caught in the crevice where the rock had slipped, was giving the man the opportunity he wanted. "Run, Linda," he panted . . .

MYSTERY
ON
GRAVEYARD
HEAD

Originally published as
NO MOON ON GRAVEYARD HEAD

EDITH DORIAN

WILDSIDE PRESS

Map by Forrest Orr

1 • *Changes On Juniper Point*

STEVE PURCHAS finished tamping earth around the last cedar post and crawled out from under the old fishhouse at the head of the family wharf. After inching around like a measuring worm for the last three hours, he was glad just to get his shoulders straight again. Besides, it had been hot enough to parboil him under there away from the breeze, and he wanted a swim. Strolling into the fishhouse, he changed his muddy dungarees for swimming trunks and ambled down to the float at the end of the wharf.

This afternoon he and the gulls had the Purchas Boat Basin to themselves. It was what Maine people call a blue-and-gold day, with deep water in Casco Bay rippling bluer than the sky in the sunshine, and most of the summer sailors had their boats out. Steve could count a dozen empty mooring buoys bobbing in the swell of the incoming tide, and with his father and Wait Webber both away, even the family boatshop was deserted. Diving into the water, he raced out to the black spar and back at top speed. Sticking a foot in Casco Bay any day was the quickest way to cool off that he had ever discovered, and right now Purchas Basin had apparently been kept in somebody's refrigerator until he hit it. Staying in ice

5

water to gambol around like a lamb on an Easter card was all right if you liked it, but it was not Steve's notion of pleasure.

He hauled himself up on the float again in a hurry and sprinted for the fishhouse. Maybe I'd better get a move on, he thought when he looked at his watch. His father and mother had driven to the Brunswick Station to bring back the people who had rented his grandfather's house for the summer. Dr. Cobb and his daughter were due in Juniper Point practically any minute, and it occurred to Steve rather belatedly that his mother would think something slightly more formal than bathing trunks was indicated for his first meeting with Miss Cobb. He yanked on a clean T-shirt and the flannel slacks he had brought along as he came down to work after dinner, and ran a pocket comb hastily through his red hair.

But there was no sign of the family Ford when he emerged from the fishhouse so he roamed on across the Point to see whether the carpenters had finally managed to shingle the one completed wing of the building under construction on the east shore. Steve had a stake in that wing, and he eyed the completed roof with approval. Those shingles meant that he was employed as of tomorrow, July first, instead of having to fiddle around until Dr. Cobb's office and workshop were made usable. At present, the other buildings planned were only holes in the ground, but by the end of August, when they would be finished, the whole setup would be the Carriker Marine Biological Laboratory; and next summer would see it in full operation.

Steve prowled interestedly around the laboratory site. With college ahead of him, he needed a summer job, and it was unexpected luck to have a full-time one develop almost on his own doorstep. Generally he was a Jack-of-all-trades, patching garage roofs, painting houses, helping to dig wells, and mowing grass for the summer people whose cottages were sprinkeld along the road and the shores of Harpswell Neck. Probably he would not be much more than a Jack-of-all-trades this summer either, but off and on this spring he had seen enough of Dr. Cobb, the lab's research director, to decide that he would like working for him.

A few die-hard old-timers who sat around Randall's Store argued that the laboratory was the worst tomfool nonsense that had hit South Harpswell yet; but in Steve's opinion, if the Purchases could stand the laboratory on Juniper Point, where nobody except their own family had lived for two hundred years, the rest of the town would survive comfortably. As a matter of fact, it had taken Dr. Cobb nearly six months to persuade Captain and Mrs. Purchas to part with land for the proposed Carriker Laboratory. Like a lot of others, they had agreed from the first that a marine biological laboratory was a thoroughly sound idea, but they had decided objections to its construction on their property. To Captain Peletiah, good fences still made good neighbors; and, for Juniper Point, Purchas Basin and Bar Island Cove were good fences. He wanted to keep any neighbors on the far side of those coves, not to have them moving in on top of him, especially if they were part-time summer residents. In the end, however, their increasing respect for both Dr. Cobb and the laboratory project had made the Captain and his wife capitulate; but Steve knew that they were still occasionally uneasy.

He frowned a little, remembering the long family discussions through the winter months. He had got a job

7

because of the laboratory and he admired Dr. Cobb; but it was hard to imagine Juniper Point with summer people underfoot all day every day. Now that the time had actually come, he was uncomfortable himself. Then suddenly he began to grin. What was he worrying about? Over across Bar Island Cove his brother Bob's best friend, Seth Green, was burying a load of trash in the Colony rubbish pit. Next winter Seth would be a senior at Bowdoin; this July he was claiming to be the only college-educated garbage man in the state of Maine. If Seth could manage to work for a dozen different summer families at the Colony, he ought to make out all right with only one. This Miss Cobb was supposed to spend most of her days wandering off with a paintbox anyway. She certainly wouldn't get in his hair so long as she didn't get any idea that he was her personal errand boy just because he worked for her father.

A raucous blast set the echoes grumbling and started Steve down the path that twisted its roundabout way along the shore through stands of pine and birch back to Purchas Basin. That horn meant that Wait Webber, his father's right-hand man, was tying the *Maquoit* up at the wharf and wanted help unloading the crates of stuff he had picked up in Portland for Dr. Cobb's office. At the same time, off beyond the bend in the Point road, Steve finally heard his father's car rattling over the planks across the salt marsh, but he did not bother to change his course. He could dust off his best manners after he had lent Waity a hand.

Jogging through the woods, he rounded the tip of Juniper Point to walk up the west shore. Well ahead of him, past the fishhouse, he could see Waity manipulating the *Maquoit's* hand winch, methodically hooking

8

big crates on its arm and swinging them over to the landing. Exactly what happened next Steve was never quite sure, but he thought Waity started the arm with a heavy load toward shore and failed to get out of its path when he straightened up. At any rate, the crate caught him full on the back of the head, and he toppled overboard like a lumpy sack of potatoes.

Steve's feet pounded on the path. The water at the landing was deep, for his father and grandfather had had Purchas Basin blasted out years ago, and Waity had gone over without even a grunt. He must have been unconscious, and with the currents eddying around the wharf, he was likely to get wedged in the pilings.

Steve ran desperately. Right now the distance between himself and the landing float seemed twice as long as usual. All that he hoped was that his father or Dr. Cobb had happened to see the accident; one of them might be nearer. He couldn't tell what was going on now that the fishhouse was beginning to block his view, but suddenly he heard feet running down the wharf. Then he was tearing around the building himself and racing out to the float. Ripples warned him that the other person had dived in, and he checked himself a second to take a hasty look. There was no sense in fouling things up by landing on somebody's back, but there was not even a shadow under him. Kicking off his shoes, he went over in a long dive.

To the right, a little below him, someone was struggling to pull Waity loose from the piling, and Steve went down fast to help. Catching the unconscious man under the arms, he shoved him forward so his wedged foot could be freed. Then, with Waity supported between them, the pair of rescuers shot to the surface. Brawny arms thrust

9

an oar within Steve's grasp, and Captain Purchas hauled them alongside the float where he and Dr. Cobb lifted Waity out and began to work over him.

Steve started to turn to see if his companion needed help, but his mother was ahead of him, her hand already outstretched, and he climbed out on the float to sit there panting. The other person flopped, dripping, beside him.

"I'm Linda Cobb," she said between gasps. "I guess you're Steve Purchas. Hi!"

2 • Trouble Off Haddock

STEVE stared at the girl on the float as if some weird fish with a couple of tails had suddenly landed beside him. This was not the kind of Miss Cobb he had been expecting to meet. Somewhere along the line, the Purchases had got it into their heads that Linda Cobb was near his brother Tom's age, and Tom was through college, married, and in the Navy. Steve tried hastily to figure out where they had gone wrong. On his flying visits to the Point, Dr. Cobb had never had occasion to talk much about his own affairs. All he had said was that he was a widower and that his daughter would be coming along with him to keep house and do some painting. It was that housekeeping business that had thrown them off, Steve realized. He started pulling himself together. Even waterlogged, Linda Cobb was easy to take, but by

10

now she probably thought he had been born with his eyes out on stilts like a lobster.

Linda chuckled at his expression. "Don't bother trying to explain," she said. "It's all Dad's fault. Your mother told me he pulled me out of his hat without any vital statistics. He's always doing it. Last summer our landlord had a playpen for me!"

Steve grinned and gave her a hand up. At least, she had a sense of humor. But with Waity on their minds, they had no time for casual conversation, and they stood, watching anxiously as Dr. Cobb continued artificial respiration. Captain Pel, though, looked up long enough to be encouraging.

"He's coming around," he said comfortably. "Stirred some a minute ago. You two go get dry. And step on it, will you, Steve? You'll have to drive over to the Neck for Dr. Littlefield. We'd better play safe."

He turned his attention back to Waity, and Steve dashed off with a muttered apology to Linda for his desertion. Throwing on dry clothes didn't take long. Linda was just disappearing through the Cobbs' front door when he slid under the wheel of the car and headed off the Point. But it was nearly six-thirty before he located a supperless Dr. Littlefield out on a call, and piloted the Ford home again, the doctor in his own car close behind him.

"Waity was on the landing float when I left," Steve said as they climbed out in front of the house. "Maybe we'd better go down there."

But his mother, on the lookout at the door, beckoned to them. "This way, Doctor," she called. "Waity's rolled up in blankets on the living-room couch. He seems pretty comfortable. And, Steve, Dad says you'd better get

11

those crates on the float under shelter for the night. The wind's shifting."

She followed the doctor into the house, and Steve went reluctantly back to the landing. At the moment, he would have been willing to call it a day without hauling a batch of heavy crates up a gangplank and along a wharf to a fishhouse. The job was finished eventually, however, and he whistled his way to the house once more, his mind fixed on his belated supper until he spotted the doctor's car still parked where they had left it. Then he took the porch steps two at a time and bolted through the hall into the living room. There was always the chance that Waity had been injured more seriously than anyone supposed.

But Waity was obviously doing fine in spite of the huge goose egg on the back of his head and the quantity of salt water that had been rolled out of him. Propped against the pillows of the couch, he was busy with a bowl of hot soup while the rest of them ate supper at a table pulled over in front of the fire. Steve tackled his own chowder, smiling with relief.

"Whew," he said. "For a minute there, I thought Dr. Littlefield had turned up a couple of broken ribs and a punctured lung."

The doctor laughed. "You can stop worrying, son. The patient'll live. Just concentrate on this supper while it's hot."

Actually, his only real concern was over the foot that Waity had caught in the piling. It was too swollen and discolored for the doctor to be sure no bones were broken, and he insisted Waity stay off it until he could drive him to Brunswick next morning for an X ray.

"You can cart him home and get him into his own

12

bed," he told the Purchases as he got ready to leave after supper. "I'll send Abby Beamish along to take care of him." Then he smiled broadly at Waity's outraged growl. "Oh, all right, have Steve if you'd rather. Only keep off that foot, Wait Webber, or I refuse to be responsible."

Smothering a laugh, Steve strolled off to collect his pajamas and toothbrush. Offhand, he couldn't think of any occasion when Abby Beamish and Wait Webber had seen eye to eye. Besides, the idea of a woman bustling around his house would raise Waity's blood pressure to an all-time high. As Harpswell's most determined bachelor, he lived alone and liked it. Steve, with an increased respect for the medical profession, helped his father carry him out to the car. Between satisfaction at escaping Abby and the sedatives administered for the pain in his ankle, Wait was obeying orders with abnormal meekness.

Steve took a quick look as they passed his grandfather's old house, but there were no Cobbs in sight. He had been at the landing moving crates when they stopped to inquire for Waity, and he had yet to see Linda without her hair plastered to her head and water dripping off her nose. But from where he sat, Linda Cobb was not hard on the eyes, wet or dry, and since she had turned out to be seventeen, the summer could have been rough if she had shown up looking like a sculpin.

The weather next morning was not calculated to lure anyone outside his own door, and there was still no sign of Linda when Steve tramped back to Juniper Point. It was already after ten o'clock. A southeaster in the night had stirred up a kettle of pea soup that made the foghorn on Halfway Rock Light wail like a banshee, and with visibility beyond ten feet absolutely nil, Dr. Littlefield had been understandably slow getting around to Ash Point to pick up his patient. Steve stopped at the house just long enough to leave his pajamas and to answer his mother's questions. Then he strode on to Purchas Landing. He still had to finish the unloading job that the accident had interrupted.

The *Maquoit,* tied up at the float the way Waity had left her, looked like a boat daubed on a backdrop that somebody had forgotten to fill in with scenery. As he climbed aboard to open up her hatch and clear her winch, Steve could hear his father's power saw whining through planks in the boatshop at the head of the cove, but for all he could see, the shop might have been at the bottom of Casco Bay. It was certainly no day for pleasure cruising. He swung the winch arm montonously back and forth, picking up crates and dumping them on the float until he had emptied the *Maquoit's* hold and could begin to haul the stuff across the Point to Dr. Cobb's office.

It was dull work, though, and he was glad to see the end of it when he manhandled his final load onto the wheelbarrow and stopped at the fishhouse to get a hammer and crowbar from the tool rack. At least, yanking the slats off the crates would keep him inside the lab wing long enough to let the fog evaporate out of his ears. He picked up the wheelbarrow handles and shoved off again. After six round trips, he felt as if he could run the course with his eyes closed, so he butted the office door open with his shoulder and backed in without bothering to look around. The possibility of traffic complications was the last thing worrying him until he pinned somebody against the wall. Then he turned in a hurry to find Linda laughing at him.

"I was going to honk," she said, "but you didn't give me time."

14

Steve chuckled. "You can't say the Purchases don't make an effort," he told her. "When we can't drown our tenants the first day, we try to flatten 'em out the next."

"You can have 'A' for effort," Linda retorted, "but you were licked before you started. The Cobbs bounce up like rubber." She eyed the crate on the wheelbarrow interestedly. "Is that the weapon that clouted Waity yesterday?"

Steve nodded. "and if it had been handy, I'd probably have bounced it off his skull again this morning," he admitted. "The easiest way to handle Wait Webber is to have him out flat counting stars. He roared around like a walrus cussing the weather from six o'clock on."

"Then I hope he did some for me," Linda said plaintively. "The first morning I've ever spent in Maine and what do I get? Visibility unlimited—clear to the end of my nose!"

She twisted around to study the wet white blanket outside the window, and Steve glanced appreciatively at her profile. He had seen plenty of worse views. In fact, this morning in charcoal dungarees and a red flannel .shirt, Linda Cobb was likely to improve any scenery he'd met. Parking lazily on the nearest crate, she watched him pry off slats until he happened to look up again and smile. Then she reached for the hammer.

"Oh, all right. You shame me into it. I'll pull the nails out of these things while you pry off the rest. I suppose you want them stacked in that wood basket, too, while I'm at it!"

She buckled to work energetically, but now and then her eyes wandered to the window for another look at the weather.

"It's positively spooky outside," she exclaimed. "Why, anything could happen in weather like this. Look at that

15

fog drift into queer shapes. I almost saw pirates landing gold a minute ago, or maybe they were smugglers loaded down with jade!"

Steve grinned at her. "Keep right on seeing things," he said. "That's all the excitement you're likely to get around here. If you wanted Indians and buccaneers, you should have dropped in a couple of hundred years ago. Kidd cruised in the Bay, and a lot of others buried gold on the Islands. My grandfather ued to tell us about a Bailey Island man who dug up twelve thousand dollars' worth of Spanish doubloons."

"When do we dig?" Linda demanded, and Steve laughed.

"We're a hundred years too late for that, too. Everybody else beat us to it. Of course, Dad says things got pretty lively again in rumrunning days, but Harpswell's turned respectably dull. My brother Bob's an ensign on one of the two coast guard cutters that get assigned to the Bay in case of trouble, and we haven't even seen the *Yakatak's* stern since he's been aboard."

Linda wagged her head sadly. "Another one of those realists," she said. "They're always taking the fun out of life. Go ahead and play it your own way. I'll keep my weather eye out for sinister ships and suspicious characters. When I'm sniffing on the trail of the treasure, you'll eat your words."

"I won't have time then," Steve said promptly. "I'll be too busy streaking past you with my shovel!"

Still laughing, Linda was tossing her armful of slats into the wood basket when voices outside shouted for Steve, and Captain Pel and Dr. Cobb hurried into the room.

"I need you, Steve," his father explained. "Some radio

16

'ham' picked up an SOS from a cruiser off Haddock Rock. Ed Randall just phoned in from the store. Let's get going. Ed's notifying the Coast Guard we'll take over with the *Abenaki*."

Steve was already on his feet, grabbing his jacket, but he stared at his father in surprise. "The *Abenaki*? With Waity laid up? What'll you do if I have to get aboard the cruiser?"

"Make out," the captain told him. "Dr. Cobb's volunteered to come along. We may be shorthanded on her, weather like this, but Ed says the cruiser's a seventy-footer. The *Maquoit* couldn't touch her with a sea on."

He turned impatiently to the door, anxious to get started, but Linda ran after him.

"Would I just be in the way, Captain Pel?" she asked. "Because I'll come if you think I'll do."

His hand on the knob, the captain regarded her quizzically. "Ever get seasick, young lady?" he demanded, and Linda shook her head.

"I don't think so," she told him. "At least, I never have when Dad's taken me out on lab boats."

"Then you're signed on," he said, and led the way rapidly down to the wharf.

3 • *The Delight Makes Port*

MRS. PURCHAS was already on the float, stowing boxes of sandwiches and a couple of quart thermos bottles of coffee in a skiff when Captain Pel and his crew came down the gangplank.

"Enough for lunch and plenty to spare if the people on the cruiser need it," she told them briskly. "And the barometer's rising, Pel. Perhaps the fog'll lift by the time you get outside the harbor."

She pulled off her slicker, nevertheless, and wrapped it around Linda. "Good luck," she called as they shoved off. "Good hunting."

Linda, seated in the stern, turned her head to smile, but Purchas Landing had faded into the fog behind them as quickly as Steve's oars dipped in the lobsterman's short, choppy strokes. With a dozen more, her bearings were gone completely. We could be rowing in circles for all I'd know, she thought, and Steve Purchas acts like a homing pigeon! Another dozen or two and the *Abenaki* was practically dead ahead of them. Linda could already see a vague green hull, shrouded in mist.

"Tie the skiff on the mooring, Steve, and cast us off," his father ordered as they drew alongside. "We'll take care of the anchor." He climbed aboard and leaned hastily over the rail. "Here, Linda, let me give you a hand up. Steve'll be along in a minute with instructions."

He and Dr. Cobb strode toward the stern, leaving her stranded amidships until Steve hit the deck five minutes later. But he was beckoning even before he headed for the engines, and she trailed willingly at his heels.

"Your father gets this engine job, once the anchor's up," he explained. "Dad'll take the wheel. You and I draw the towing gear." His hand on the throttle, he listened to the rattle of chains from the stern, waiting for his father's signal. "We'll be working back there, too," he said. "We only have to stick around here till your father takes over."

Finally a bell sounded from the wheelhouse forward, and Steve got the engines moving. Then Dr. Cobb was at hand to check briefly with Steve before he assumed his responsibilities, and the younger members of the crew headed aft to tackle their own job. Working together, they opened up stern lockers and began to ready gear. "Boat hooks, too, Linda," Steve said, and went on dragging out heavy coils of cable as she hunted them up. Though he hadn't taken time off to say so, he thoroughly approved of having her along. For the second time in two days Linda was coming in handy in an emergency.

Often a crewman from the rescue ship was needed on a disabled craft, and Steve knew that he might have to return aboard their tow. Linda was no Wait Webber in a crew; still, without her on the way back, Dr. Cobb might have been saddled with the winch and the towing gear, in addition to the engines. A man could manage a lot of things simultaneously when he had to, of course, but it might have been strenuous. Towing cables had parted before this.

Hawk-eyed, Steve examined every inch of the cables before he shoved two aside in case of trouble, and turned back to Linda.

"We'll thread a couple on the winch," he told her. "This cruiser's heavy and we'll probably need them both. Can you hang on to this stuff and feed it to me?"

Linda nodded, and they struggled with the salt-stiffened cables, not evey trying to talk, their thoughts on the cruiser somewhere ahead of them in the fog. But the barometer really had meant business, the girl decided, when Steve made her take a minute off to rest her hands and she had a chance to look around. She could see half a dozen boats on their moorings, in the harbor now and make out the blurred outlines of the long wharf where the Casco Bay Line's *Aucocisco* docked on her trips to and from Portland. Back in Purchas Basin all that she had been able to see was the water under their own bow.

"Is Haddock Rock far from us?" she asked.

Steve shook his head. "Not in miles, but too far for that cruiser's comfort. This fog's been slowing us like crazy, and the *Abenaki*'s no race horse at best." He pointed at the jagged, weed-covered ledges stretching down into the Bay off Harpswell Neck. "Nasty things to pile up on," he said soberly, "and the cruiser's got plenty of them to worry her out behind Haskell Island."

They went back to their job on the winch. Time was getting shorter. Now that the visibility was improving by the minute, Captain Pel had begun to drive the *Abenaki* hard through the heavy seas. The storm that had blown through the night and early morning had left the Bay in turmoil. Even in the shelter of the harbor, they had felt the force of the swells under their ship's keel, and out here beyond the end of Potts Point she fought head on against the rising tide.

His father was holding their course straight out for deep water off Haskell, Steve noticed, as they finished their job and hurried forward to join the others around the wheel for a hasty lunch. Apparently he was calculating the effect of wind and tide on the cruiser's drift.

Captain Pel nodded when he saw his son's glance.

"There was no sense in working through the Gut and running along the outside shore," he said. "That 'ham' thought the cruiser's engines were dead so she's more'n likely drifted up this way—if she isn't hung up on a

20

ledge somewhere." He sounded troubled. "Tide's turned and the weight of the wind's behind it. There'll be a sea off Haskell."

Linda blinked at him. What did he call this? With the *Abenaki* pitching headlong, it didn't seem like a duck pond to her. But when they finally ran out from the protection of the farthest headland, she knew what he had meant. The *Abenaki* stopped pitching and began to buck like a rodeo bronco. Then Steve gave a shout and she forgot the ship's antics to race to the rail. Between the ragged ledges of Haskell Island and Haddock Rock, they had found the cruiser wallowing heavily, broadside to the incoming seas. Steve just made out the name and port across her stern as the *Abenaki*, engines throttled down, nosed into hailing distance.

"*Delight,* Palm Beach," he said to Linda. "Great guns, she's come a long way to find trouble!"

The four men aboard the *Delight* cheered them heartily. "Our second anchor, on chain, parted ten minutes ago." It was the broad-shouldered man with the iron-gray hair who shouted to them. "Can you shoot us a line, *Abenaki?* We're using a drag but we're drifting in fast."

Captain Pel nodded. "Stand by," he called. "We're dropping a cable in your bow."

Braced in the stern, Steve waited while the *Abenaki* forged slowly ahead. Then, with one tremendous heave, he shoved the coiled ends of the heavy towing cables onto the deck of the cruiser and sprang down to take care of his end of the operations at the winch.

The gray-haired man smiled his thanks. "My name's Sutton. Dr. Bartley Sutton." He raised his voice as the water widened between the two boats. "We're mighty grateful to you." Lifting an arm in salute, he turned quickly away to lend his men a hand.

Steve knew that his father would idle the *Abenaki*'s engines as long as he dared, and he kept his eyes on the *Delight*'s crew, approvingly gauging their speed with the towlines. Every second counted now. At Captain Pel's quiet orders, Dr. Cobb sent their engines inching ahead again and again to counteract their own drift, but with each wind-driven wave they could see the *Delight* roll perceptibly closer to the ledges. No improvised drag could possibly hold the big cruiser long in a sea as heavy as this. The four on the Purchas ship, waiting grimly for some word that the towlines were secured, felt ready to cheer when Dr. Sutton sprang into the *Delight*'s bow, signaling with his arms, and Captain Pel could get cautiously under way.

Steve and Linda stayed together in the stern, nursing the towing gear. Even a greenhorn like Linda could see that they were not out of trouble. If those towlines parted, their difficulties would start all over again; yet they had to haul the *Delight* clear of Haskell before there would be leeway to circle out for the return trip. Fighting the tide in a rough sea, with the heavy cruiser dragging, was slow, grueling work for the *Abenaki*. This was not like towing in the open sea with a long length of line paid out behind you. Here you had to shorten lines to keep your tow off the reefs, and the strain on the cables increased proportionately. Steve sat tense and tight-lipped, ready to shout a warning to his father, until the laboring *Abenaki* rounded the island and had wind and tide behind her to ease the cables' strain.

"Look, we're actually moving again!" Linda exclaimed. "I began to think this Bay was filled with glue."

Steve grinned and relaxed a little. "Some job," he said feelingly. "That's what we get for being nearer than the Coast Guard this time. You pulled your weight, Linda. It was a smart idea to bring you along."

The girl's face flushed with pleasure. "At least I didn't get seasick," she said, laughing, "so I guess I passed your father's test."

They sat in companionable silence for a while. Behind them in the *Delight*, Dr. Sutton and his crew were spelling each other, two of them manning the towlines and two resting, turn and turn about. After their battle with high seas in the helpless cruiser, they were exhausted.

"I wonder who Dr. Sutton is," Steve said finally. "One thing sure, he's not starving, not with a plaything like that cruiser. I hope he sticks around long enough to let us get aboard."

"Well, he can't get very far till his engines are fixed," Linda pointed out. "We've got him in our clutches for a few days anyway. I've always wanted to see a ship's galley."

Reminded of food, she rummaged around for the sandwiches she had put aside and set the open box between them. "There wasn't any sense in passing these over to that cruiser," she said, biting into deviled ham contentedly. "That man bringing out the coffeepot back there now must be the cook."

"Could be," Steve agreed. "Even the luxury liner behind us doesn't need more than two in her crew when her owner's his own skipper." Again he eyed the big cruiser with admiration. "She's a beauty all right."

Eventually, the *Abenaki* worked her slow way past the tip of Harpswell Neck, and Captain Pel called Steve forward.

"Shorten those cables still more," he told his son. "I'm not aiming to run foul of the *Petticoat* or the *Delilah* or any other craft in the harbor with that dancing tow. She's as skittish as a porpoise. And stand by, Steve, in case of trouble."

But the cruiser behaved like a lady, once Steve and the winch had worked her in closer, and they threaded their way through the harbor without any incidents.

Leaning out of his store window, Ed Randall waved cheerfully as they passed Town Landing; and in home waters, when they reached at last for their mooring, they could see Deborah Purchas flapping a dish towel in triumph on the back porch. The *Delight* was safe in port.

4 · Jude Farr's Grandson

THE Purchas kitchen was fragrant with the buttery smell of lobster stew when the rescue crew came through the doorway, bringing Dr. Sutton with them. Mrs. Purchas, busy sliding pans of rolls into the oven, stopped to greet their guests warmly.

"I've nearly worn the binoculars out watching for the *Abenaki*," she said, smiling. "It's good to know you're safe. Supper will be ready by the time you've had a chance to catch your breath, and Wait Webber will be hobbling in to join us any minute. He's been down at the boatshop a couple of hours."

"With that foot!" Steve exclaimed disgustedly. "Is he crazy?"

His mother's eyes twinkled. "He sounded pretty normal to me," she admitted. "He spent fifteen minutes here in the kitchen sampling stew and taking doctors apart for the way they cramp your style with adhesive. He's all right, Steve. There weren't any bones broken. Dr. Littlefield dropped him off himself."

She turned pleasantly back to their guest. "You and the *Delight* took care of today, Doctor," she explained, "but Waity provided yesterday's excitement. When the Cobbs saw him, he was half-drowned."

"A mite of water in my scuppers," Waity agreed, limping into the room, "but I don't know if it wasn't a sight better'n being checkreined and harnessed so tight the beach fleas play tag all over me."

Mrs. Purchas presented him to Dr. Sutton and the Cobbs, and he stared down in obvious surprise at Linda's head, a good four inches below his shoulder. "I've been wanting to say 'much obliged' for pulling me out," he assured her. "Only thing now, I'm kind of sorry I missed that performance." Waity shook his head regretfully. "Must have been considerable like watching a herring try to tow a shark."

They were a contented group when they gathered around the supper table, and Dr. Sutton, of course, was the center of everyone's attention. Long before they had reached doughnuts and coffee, he had had to tell the story of the failing engines and the heavy seas that had nearly ended in disaster for the *Delight*. It made thrilling listening.

"I'd have been petrified," Linda confessed at the end. "I can't even decide which part was worst."

25

"I can manage quite nicely without a repeat performance of any of it," Dr. Sutton told her, "but that last hour off Haddock Rock when our anchors parted, first one and then the other, finished eight of my nine lives."

"Enough to take your mind off blueberry picking," Waity agreed, and Dr. Sutton laughed.

"It certainly was," he said. "As a matter of fact, I never expect to see a prettier sight than the *Abenaki* nosing around the end of Haskell Island!"

"The Bay doesn't always treat strangers that way," Mrs. Purchas said apologetically, "so we hope you'll stay long enough to fall under her spell in spite of a bad beginning."

"Actually, I'm planning to stay the rest of the summer," Dr. Sutton said, "I hadn't got around to telling you, but I own an old house somewhere here in Harpswell. It belonged to a family named Farr."

Captain Pel snapped his fingers with satisfaction. "That's the answer, of course," he exclaimed. "Your name has been teasing at my mind all afternoon, Doctor. So you're one of the Sutton family those Boston lawyers have been handling taxes for all these years!" He looked across at the doctor with fresh interest. "If I recollect rightly, my father used to say Jude Farr had a distant cousin surviving somewhere out West. You're kin to him, I take it."

Dr. Sutton shook his head. "Not kin to him," he explained, "kin to Jude Farr and his wife Patience. My mother was their daughter."

The Purchases and Wait Webber looked at him in blank bewilderment. "You're claiming to be Jude Farr's grandson?" Captain Pel put down his coffee cup as if it were suddenly too heavy to hold. "Why, Jude and

26

Patience never had but the one child, and she was lost, along with them, when their ship went down in a gale off the coast of Florida."

He pushed back his chair and reached for a big scrapbook on the shelves behind him. "I forget the date—it was before my time, but the newspaper story's pasted in here. My father kept everything he found in print about Harpswell ships and Harpswell seamen."

The others crowded around to look over Captain Pel's shoulder as he laid the book down and turned the pages.

"There," he said, pointing to a yellowed clipping, "the ship that foundered was Jude's own *Sturdy Beggar,* and the date was 1902."

Nodding, Dr. Sutton brought his wallet out of his pocket and extracted another yellowed clipping to lay beside the first.

"The story has a sequel," he told them, "a happy ending. Delight Farr did survive. A life preserver and some drifting wreckage kept her afloat, but she was ill for a long time after a fishing smack picked her up and brought her into Palm Beach. She had been pretty badly battered about the head, Dad said. It was months before she remembered who she was or what ship she had sailed in."

He put a snapshot of a handsome man and woman on top of the clippings. "Joel Haine Sutton and Delight Farr Sutton." He showed them the names on the back. "Delight married the young doctor who took care of her during her illness. I was their only child."

The group around Captain Pel still looked at Dr. Sutton in amazement. "It's like something out of a book," Linda said wonderingly. "It's not what happens to people you actually know."

Then Captain Pel and Wait were shaking hands again with Dr. Sutton, and Mrs. Purchas was beaming.

"So you're really going to open the old Farr house," she exclaimed with satisfaction. "I've never seen it alive —just dead and dreary looking. Houses aren't meant to be like that."

Dr. Sutton smiled as though he understood what had troubled her. "Mother felt the same way," he said. "That's one reason I've come. My father had a Boston law firm take charge of everything. They shipped family papers down to Mother and had the house boarded up. She hated thinking of it like that. When I was small, she was always planning to spend summers here as soon as my father could take real vacations. She never had the opportunity; she died before I finished grade school." The doctor shook his head ruefully. "I meant to get here myself years ago, but it was hard for a young surgeon to steal a lengthy holiday. Fifty years, though, is a long time for a house to be deserted. I'll be lucky now, I suppose, if the timbers aren't rotten."

"Timbers are sound enough," Captain Pel told him. "I was over that way duck hunting in the fall and prowled around some. Your mother probably told you that the Farr place was a garrison house originally; the old walls are eighteen inches thick. Shingles and porches, the barn ell, too—those are what will need attention."

"Maybe a few spring cleanings wouldn't have hurt much either," Mrs. Purchas suggested mildly.

Dr. Sutton whistled. "Great Scott, I never thought of dirt," he admitted. "It must be a foot deep!"

Grinning wickedly, Steve glanced out of the corner of his eye at Waity. "You get Abby Beamish after it, Dr. Sutton," he advised. "Abby says there's no percentage

28

in everyday cleaning; she likes dirt enough to begin on to know she's done something when she's through."

Waity snorted, and Steve smiled. "Just don't go buying her a lot of newfangled cleaning apparatus though," he warned the doctor. "Waity bought a broom down at Randall's last week, and I heard Abby telling him a new broom might sweep clean but the old one knew where the dirt hid."

Dr. Sutton laughed outright. "The redoubtable Miss Beamish it is then," he announced. "How do I go about luring the lady into my cobwebs?"

"Mrs., not Miss." Waity was still snorting when he corrected him. "Dirt'll do the luring, Dr. Sutton; don't you trouble your head about that. You've got self-preservation to fret over. Dirt lured her into Lem Beamish's place eight years ago, and before Lem knew what was happening, Abby'd married him." Waity looked owlish. "Come spring, she'd cleaned Lem Beamish straight into the graveyard. If you've a mite of sense, you'll take out over the clam flats and let Abby Beamish lie."

But the doctor refused to be daunted. "You've got to admit I'm prepared," he told him. "That's more than Lem was."

Mrs. Purchas's eyes danced. "Prepared?" she repeated. "My stars, you're practically barricaded in the cruiser's cabin with your diving suit at hand! If Abby Beamish needs a cake of soap, she'll have to rout out the Coast Guard to find you."

Still laughing, she stacked the dishes on a tray to start for the kitchen, but Dr. Sutton reached persuasively for the sweater hanging on the back of her chair.

"Those dishes have the patience of Job," he insisted. "Daylight hasn't, and I've come a thousand miles to see

29

a house. There must be a car around here somewhere."

"A new station wagon in our barn," Dr. Cobb offered promptly, and Mrs. Purchas untied her apron.

"I'm already on my way," she said. But she paused a second as she started for the door. "Pel, please go find a hammer and a crowbar. Dr. Sutton's going to have a chance to see the boards off the door over on Graveyard Head if I never wash those dishes."

5 • The House On Graveyard Head

WHEN Linda slid into the back seat of the station wagon with Steve, she still thought her ears had been playing her tricks.

"Your mother didn't really say *Graveyard Head,* did she?"

"Sure she said Graveyard Head. That's the name of the headland where the Farr house is." Steve chuckled at Linda's incredulous face. "Cheerful sort of address, isn't it?"

"But why?" Linda demanded. "For goodness' sake, why?"

"Because the Farrs put their graveyard along the shore at the top of the ledges," Steve explained. "You couldn't miss it from the water. It's all tangled up in vines and bayberry bushes so you can hardly find it now, but Grandfather said ships beating up Merriconeag Sound in the old days used to steer their course by the Farr headstones."

"I still don't get it," Linda said in bewilderment. "Why didn't they use a cemetery like other people?"

"But there wasn't any regular burying ground when the Farrs settled here," Steve told her. "All the early settlers had family graveyards, and a lot of them kept on using them even after they built a Meetinghouse in 1758. You would have, too, if you'd had to lug a heavy coffin five miles over rough trails to the church ground in Center Harpswell."

Linda laughed. "Maybe I would, though I'd never have guessed it if you hadn't told me. I can't seem to picture families living in the same house in the same place hundreds of years. Down home in New York hardly anybody we know was even born in the city. Anyway, if I'd been a Farr, I'd have got rid of that graveyard name in a hurry."

Steve grinned at her. "You'd have had a swell job on your hands. Fifty years from now Grandfather's house will still be the 'Lorenzo Purchas place' even if Dad suddenly sells it to you tomorrow. Besides, the name fits. Wait till you get a look at that house on the Head."

By that time, the station wagon was turning out of Juniper Point and starting along the main road on Harpswell Neck. Dr. Cobb barely crawled. Half his carload was giving him direcions while they hunted for the break in a tangle of bushes that marked the old entrance to Dr. Sutton's property.

"There it is, about ten feet in front of you." Captain Pel pointed to the right of the road. "Better park where you are, Dr. Cobb. There's no earthly use trying to turn in on the Head. Dr. Sutton'll need a bulldozer before a car'll navigate that road again. There's a footpath, though; duck hunters and berrypickers have kept it open after a fashion."

Following his lead, they plunged through the bushes, strung out in single file. Steve and Linda brought up the rear. Bayberry thickets and scrub growth hemmed them in on both sides, and overhead, wind-twisted birches nearly locked branches. Linda hardly took a step without turning an ankle or getting tangled up in blackberry creepers.

"Those Farrs certainly had sense," she admitted. "I'd have made two graveyards right under my front porch before I'd carry anything bigger than a pillbox over a trail like this. You don't suppose Waity would like to lend me that nice stiff horse collar he's got on his ankle, do you? His foot's the only one that's safe."

But the narrow rutted path finally opened into a pine woods where the traces of the old road were easier to follow.

"Going'll be better in a minute," Captain Pel promised. "The Head's so rocky it won't support much except juniper and berry bushes. That's what made it so good for a garrison in the old days—not much grass to set afire and no cover for the French and Indians."

But Linda was in no state of mind to brood over the past. She could start thinking about history if she reached Dr. Sutton's house without a broken ankle, and she continued to pick her way gingerly until she emerged intact from the woods. Then she stopped to stare across the headland at the T-shaped old Farr house, its crossbar facing south down the Bay to the open sea and its tail of barn and additions stretching northward.

"See what I meant?" Steve asked, and she nodded slowly. If there was ever a headquarters for a ghost convention, it was that gaunt, weather-beaten old place with its doors and windows boarded tight and the sea gulls roosting on its chimneys.

"Bright and cheery all right!" Steve said as they started after the others down the field. "When I was in fifth grade, a gang of us used to come over here just before dark and scare ourselves half to death. Jim Moody had nightmares all night because we dared him to stay alone on the back porch fifteen minutes."

"What did you expect him to have?" Linda demanded. "Edgar Allan Poe and Charles Addams probably dreamed that house up between them. Steve Purchas, if you get more than six inches away from me when we're inside, I know I'll drop dead and haunt you!"

But by the time the pair of them had caught up with the rest, the atmosphere around the Farr house had grown so practical that any self-respecting ghost would have taken flight, squalling, with the outraged sea gulls, from the roof. Four men were prowling from one side to another, tapping framework for the hollow tune of rotten wood, and on the front porch Mrs. Purchas was prodding and poking at the floor boards.

"They'll still hold us over there by the door," she announced. "You can get busy with that crowbar, Steve."

The sound of ripping wood brought the men hurrying up the steps, ready to lend a hand, but Steve was not having much trouble. Rusty nails and screws simply broke off under pressure. It was the door itself that presented the real problem. In the end, they had to force it because the lock was so badly corroded. Then Dr. Sutton pushed it wide, and they crowded after him, peering eagerly over one another's shoulders. Even with only the door open, light streamed ahead of them down the wide hall, and they could see how meticulously Patience Farr had prepared her home for safekeeping before she sailed on her last ill-fated voyage. Yellowed dust sheets covered settles and tables, and on the wall each picture wore a newspaper blanket.

"How Dr. Sutton's grandmother must have loved her house to take care of it this way," Linda exclaimed impulsively.

"Loved it and had to leave it again and again to sail with Jude," Mrs. Purchas said, nodding. "Just as Jude's mother before her had loved it and left it to sail the seven seas. Farrs were born at sea and died at sea, Linda, but the Head was always home."

Naturally, upstairs was too dark to explore, but they looked as best they could through every room on the first floor, barking their shins on furniture and stirring up clouds of dust, before they wandered down the hall again to the front door. The shrouded pictures on the wall had roused Linda's curiosity more than anything else.

"What do you suppose they are?" she asked Steve as the rest trooped out ahead of them.

"Family portraits and pictures of the Farr ships, I guess," he said. "Most of the old houses around here are full of them."

Sunlight was streaking across one picture right in front of them, and Linda reached up to tuck its wrapper more securely behind the frame. "Watch it," Steve warned her, but the paper had already crumbled under her touch, and she looked at him in dismay.

"Never mind," he said. "Go ahead and pull the rest off. We can wrap it up again. Waity's got tonight's paper stuck in his pocket. I'll go swipe a piece of that."

Left alone a minute, Linda removed the last dusty

34

shreds and studied the picture in delight. It was a portrait of an oddly beautiful girl with a cluster of flaming red curls in the nape of her neck and strange greenish lights in her eyes. She's only a little older than I am, Linda thought, but she's not nearly as tame. Maybe she was born in a storm at sea. She leaned forward quickly to read the name "Loraney Farr" on a brass plate. Then she rewrapped the picture in the newspaper that Steve brought her and they strolled on outside.

"You'll want electric lights and plumbing, I suppose," Dr. Cobb was saying when they found the others. "What about water? Will you drill a well?"

"If I have to, of course," Dr. Sutton said, "but there used to be a wonderful spring on the place according to my mother. Maybe one of the Purchases can tell us what's happened to it."

"You mean the Witch Spring, Dr. Sutton," Steve told him. "It's still the best spring anywhere around. I've been here berrying when it hadn't rained all summer and half the wells were dry, but the Witch was flowing the same as ever. She's over here." He led the way toward a green thicket a dozen yards further. "The springhouse tumbled down years ago though. You'll have to build that over again."

Trailing along after them, Linda listened interestedly. What she wanted to have accounted for was that name. "Would somebody please stop just long enough to tell me why it's called the 'Witch Spring'?" she asked.

"Because the Farrs were smart enough to have a witch in their family," Mrs. Purchas said, smiling. "She tapped the ground one day and created it. At least, that's the way the story goes. Before that, the Farrs had a dug well and it was always running dry like everybody else's."

35

They stood awhile watching the water flow steadily over the worn silvery stones, and Linda's eyes grew dreamy. "Perhaps she's still lurking around her spring, Dr. Sutton," she said. "Maybe if you're lucky, you'll see her riding her broomstick across the face of the moon with her nose in a big shadowy hook and her white hair flying."

"Then she won't be our witch, and I'll have to chase her for trespassing," the doctor protested. "There was nothing toothless and scraggly about the Farr witch, I'll have you know! Ours was nineteen and redheaded."

"A disturbin' woman," Waity added promptly. "That's what my great-great-grandfather called her in his diary. Loraney, her name was. She was living on Bailey Island yonder, time she married Shubael Farr."

He pointed at the rocky shore across Merriconeag Sound, but Linda was paying no attention.

"Why, I've just seen her back there at the house," she cried. "No wonder she didn't look as tame as I do."

At Dr. Sutton's startled expression, Steve couldn't keep his face straight, and Linda chuckled.

"Her picture's hanging in the hall," she explained. "She's absolutely gorgeous. I can understand Shubael all right, but what made a witch decide to capture him, Dr. Sutton? Was he supposed to be fabulous?"

"Girl in every port, according to the family stories," the doctor assured her, "but frankly I suspect Shubael was a man of business. I have his old account books, and for a whole year he'd entered regular payments to Loraney opposite the notation 'spells for favorable winds.' Perhaps he decided it would be more economical to marry his witch. Then fixing up fair winds for his voyages would fall under the head of 'wifely duties.'"

36

But Linda refused to listen. "I don't believe it," she announced indignantly. "Loraney bewitched Shubael for some good reason of her own. She brewed brews and mixed potions."

"Strawberry hair likely was enough brew," Waity said drily. "It beats all how unsettled most men can get when a redheaded woman crosses their bow."

Dr. Sutton laughed. "As long as she fixed up this spring for me, I don't mind how unsettled Shubael managed to get. Anyhow, poor Loraney's spells must have failed her. The first voyage she and Shubael sailed together, neither they nor their ship came back."

The general conversation turned to practical details of piping water into the Farr house, and Steve pulled Linda aside. "Loraney's headstone's down near the shore with the others," he said, and she fell hastily into step at his side.

"What's her headstone doing there, though, if she was lost at sea?" she demanded.

"Families put them up anyway," Steve explained. "After a ship was so long overdue they had to give up hope, they ordered a headstone with 'Lost at Sea' on it. There are plenty of that kind with nobody under them on Graveyard Head. The Farrs were all sailors—fishermen and whalers and clipper-ship men."

He pushed tangle after tangle of myrtle and wild grape aside, hunting until he found the stone that he wanted. "Here it is," he said. LORANEY. WIFE OF SHUBAEL FARR. LOST AT SEA 1798. AGED 19. The minister's supposed to have come galloping right down here to order the witch's stone pulled out, but it didn't get him anywhere. The Farrs just said they put headstones up for Farrs regardless, and that was that—except they didn't go to Meeting for quite a spell!"

Linda looked around her. At her feet slept generations of seafaring men and women. Behind her, the lilacs they had planted guarded the old wall, built stone upon stone from their rocky acres. Before her, the Bay they loved slapped little waves against ledges they had climbed.

She turned eagerly to Steve. "I hope Dr. Sutton clears away the weeds and tangles. I want the stones to be visible again so sailors on the Sound nowadays can know how much the Farrs loved the sea."

Steve looked down at her in surprise. He had not expected her to understand why the Farrs lay sleeping as close to the Bay as they could get. "We'll work on Dr. Sutton," he said. "Just lilacs and flowers aren't enough for seafaring people like them."

6 • Sea Gulls And Shingles

WHEN they came wandering back, Steve and Linda found the rest impatiently waiting for them. The sun had started to slip down behind the pines, and nobody wanted to pick his way through that overgrown footpath in the dark.

"Where did you two disappear?" Dr. Sutton asked as they began the trek to the station wagon. "Down on the beach?"

"Close to it," Steve said. "We went down to see Loraney's headstone, but it's a chore to find it. That burying ground's pretty much of a mess, Dr. Sutton. Vines and creepers and rank grass all over it. You're going to have a job resetting markers if they're not cut out of that tangle soon."

The doctor nodded. "My sins of omission are catching up with me. The list's a mile long now, and Alex Cobb says no one around here has time to hire out to work in lobster season! I'm beginning to think I should have shipped a crew of carpenters aboard the *Delight*."

"Dr. Cobb ought to know," Steve said, grinning. "People around Harpswell do their own plumbing and carpentry, and he snaked in every man who does stuff like that for the summer people. They don't go lobstering, so he still thinks he's got them sewed up full time on his lab job. Wait till he learns about haying!"

"I'll be looking forward to it," Dr. Sutton admitted. "I understand he's got you sewed up, too."

"Five days a week, tight as a button," Steve agreed.

The doctor promptly looked hopeful. "Then maybe I can get a mortgage on a couple of Saturdays and Sundays," he suggested. "The boys on the *Delight* can stand a few watches with paint buckets, and I'll scare up carpenters and paper hangers somewhere. If you'd just yank the old shingles off that roof next week end and clean out the graveyard when you get a chance, that's all I'd ask."

"It doesn't sound as if it would strain me much," Steve had to admit. "If that's all you want, I guess I can manage."

"Then that's settled," Dr. Sutton said with relief. "Use your own judgment about what to cut out down by the shore, Steve. I'll put that problem on your shoulders."

"And I'm signing on right now as foreman," Linda

39

said firmly. "If you think you're chopping out all those wild things around Loraney, Steve Purchas, you're fired already. The rest of the Farrs have to be tidy and ship-shape, of course, but her marker belongs in those tangles."

Steve studied her a second. "Worse than Shubael," he said, shaking his head. "Bewitched. Maybe you ought to get this place exorcised, Dr. Sutton. Loraney's still working spells."

But Linda refused to be baited. "Just remember I'll be watching," she said sweetly and swung around for a last look at the Head. The sun was slanting across the porch of the old garrison house, and she could almost see it catch again in the red curls of Shubael's green-eyed witch. Loraney must have stood there often, smiling over the secret things she knew.

"Oh, Dr. Sutton, I love your Headland!" Linda had forgotten that she had ever thought the Farr house grim and forbidding. "Will you let me come here and paint sometimes?"

"Paint?" the doctor asked, his interest obvious. "Any time, anywhere you like. I never could draw a line myself so I had to turn into a collector. Do you use oils or water color?"

"I use water color, but I've only been in a few classes at Cooper Union so far," she told him honestly.

The note of authority in Dr. Sutton's voice when he mentioned painting puzzled her. She looked at him again trying to think. Where had she heard of a Dr. Sutton in connection with art? Then suddenly she remembered, and her eyes opened wide.

"Dr. Sutton! You're not the man in all the newspaper

40

stories who outbid the Museum of Modern Art for those two Orrin Woods last winter, are you?"

The doctor nodded. "Guilty," he confessed, "but I can't say my conscience hurts. I'd have done a lot more than outbid a museum to get those two Woods into my possession. You use the Head as much as you like, Linda. I'll be glad to have you here."

So that's who Dr. Sutton was! Linda turned to Steve the minute their companion strode ahead to speak to Captain Pel.

"You were certainly right," she exclaimed. "Dr. Sutton's not starving any. He's one of the most famous art collectors in the country." She looked after the doctor thoughtfully. "Isn't it queer he hasn't turned up on the Head before? People do make the craziest excuses for not getting around to things, Steve. He never was the kind of young surgeon who had to earn money for a vacation. According to those newspaper stories, he inherited oil wells when he was twenty. He could have come any time he wanted to—he's always spent weeks on end in Bermuda."

Dr. Cobb dropped Waity off at his own house, and the rest of the group separated almost as soon as they got back to Juniper Point. After a day of interruptions, everyone had something to finish. Steve still had to run the *Maquoit* out to her mooring; so he walked down to the landing with Dr. Sutton. That's quite a guy, he thought as he watched the older man row over to the *Delight*. And he couldn't find anything wrong with Linda Cobb's batting average either. She'd been hitting home runs ever since she arrived. Thinking about her, he wondered how much he would actually see of Linda in the weeks ahead. The accident and the SOS had tossed them at each other, but once Juniper Point settled to the daily dozen, the situation might change. She didn't seem to be allergic to Purchases so far. Just the same, she was on vacation, and she would have more in common with the summer crowd.

He certainly saw almost nothing of her the next week. The daily dozen had taken over with a vengeance. Sea and Shore Fisheries men drove in to Juniper Point early Monday morning with an experimental project in their minds, and as a result, both Steve and Dr. Cobb were swamped. They worked all day and most of the evenings building storage cupboards and setting up equipment to convert the biologist's office into a satisfactory laboratory before the next week end. But as far as Steve could see, everyone was involved with time-consuming extras. Dr. Sutton, of course, was making Purchas Basin his headquarters while Captain Pel repaired the *Delight*, and he showed a positive genius for cajoling other people into helping him solve his problems. Mrs. Purchas was spending the major part of her days managing Abbey Beamish or inspecting sinks, stoves, and refrigerators; and afternoons, the Cobb station wagon, with Linda at the wheel, ran a shuttle service between the Brunswick shops and Graveyard Head.

Steve generally caught up with the day's events at suppertime. By Tuesday he knew Linda had already met some of the summer crowd. His mother told him she had introduced her to Seth Green and a group from the Colony on Brunswick's Maine Street, and he spotted a car with a Texas license in front of the Cobb's house the next night. After that, he expected to hear that she was swimming or playing tennis over on the other side of Bar Island Cove, but, to his surprise, she went on with her taxi

42

service. His mother was obviously distressed by the amount of time Linda was spending on the road, though. Steve had never seen her more pleased than she was Friday night when she announced that the doctor had ordered a Jeepster.

"He's got a demonstration car to use in the meantime," she told her family. "That'll free Linda, thank goodness. Not that I won't miss her," she added vigorously. "There's enough yeast in that girl to make her good company. But she's so devoted to Dr. Sutton that she's playing taxi when she ought to be painting. She's got too much talent to throw time away."

Steve remembered his mother's comments when he shoved a ladder against the Farr house Saturday morning to begin on the shingles. According to her notions, now that Dr. Sutton had a car, Linda should have been perched on the front steps with a sketch pad, working like mad. This was her first chance to paint on the Head since Jim Moody had opened up the road with his bulldozer. From his perch on the ladder, Steve looked at the road again with approval. He had not been back since the day they had towed the *Delight* into port, and mere reports of progress had not prepared him for quite so much improvement.

For an easygoing Southerner, Dr. Sutton sure get things done, Steve thought as he pried shingles off the slope of the roof above the rain barrel. Of course, his turning out to be a Farr had been no liability. Jim Moody had brought his bulldozer over for the same neighborly reasons that would have made him help raise a new house for any other year-rounder the first week end after the old one had burned. Nobody knew better than Steve that the summer resident did not yet exist, no matter how sizable

43

his bank account, who could have persuaded Jim to tackel that road after hauling lobster traps all day. The rest of the secret, however, was the doctor's friendliness. The Neck liked him on sight, summer and winter residents both.

Through an open window below, Abby Beamish's voice was tenting briskly on the old campground, and Steve chuckled to himself. Even Abby ate out of Dr. Sutton's hand. For that matter, who was he to talk? Wasn't he skidding around a roof yanking off shingles the first free day he'd had in a week?

He was going full tilt an hour later when someone's whistle sent him inching upward to pop his head over the ridgepole. Linda was down in the road, looking up at him.

"I'm parking on the ledges near the graveyard," she called. "How about bringing your lunch down when you get hungry?"

"Not a bad idea," he agreed promptly. "I'll gallop across at noon to see whether you've taken off on Loraney's broomstick. Maybe I'll get your lunch, too."

He grinned down at her and watched her black curls bob on past the house before he went back to work. When he looked at her, it was hard to take Linda's painting seriously. He knew his mother thought she was good, but when it came to Linda Cobb, his mother was transparently prejudiced. She had almost adopted the girl.

The sun was high overhead as Steve backed down the ladder, feeling as if he had earned his lunch. He had guaranteed to have the roof ready for the carpenters on Monday, and he was set to finish stripping the shingles off by the end of the afternoon. He'd have one free day out of his week end yet. Whistling contentedly, he rescued his lunch from the back porch and strolled off to

44

find Linda on her ledges. She was still there, hunched over her sketch pad, but apparently she had forgotten that food existed. Neither his whistle nor his footsteps made the slightest impression, and he banged on his tin lunch box.

"Hey," he called. "Come to. It's time to put on your feed bag."

Linda twisted around and stared up at him gloomily. "Have you ever tried to paint sea gulls?" she asked. "They keep zooming off when I want to see how they're put together."

Shoving her drawing pad disgustedly aside, she found her own lunch and settled down on the rocks.

Steve helped himself to the banana she offered. "What's the matter with your gulls?" he wanted to know.

"They look like ghosts flapping their sheets, that's what's wrong with them. Take a look for yourself if you want." She handed him the sketch pad, pointing. "Over there on the last pages. I've been practicing on them for the last hour."

Steve turned on a critical eye on the offending gulls. "They're bats," he decided candidly. "Anyway, half bat. No sea gull ever grew a wing like that, Linda. Here, wait a minute." He hunted for a pencil and turned her page over. "I can't draw worth a hoot but I can give you the idea. A gull's wings are made this way. See?" His pencil began moving across the paper. "That's the bony structure; then the wing gets attached to the body like this. Got it?"

Linda was watching attentively. "I think so," she said, "but I'd like to keep yours to study. Where on earth did you learn to do muscles and bones like that?"

"Fiddling with dead birds on the beach. It used to come

in handy for biology lab." He smiled at her, hesitant. "All right if I take a look at what you've been doing?"

Linda nodded, and he flipped back the pages on his lap, staring in surprise at the water color of the beach and the sandspit she had been working on. Steve nearly whistled. His mother was right; Linda Cobb could paint. You could almost feel the lazy motion in the water beyond her rocks.

"You've got what it takes!" he said with conviction.

There was such honest admiration in his voice that Linda's brown eyes glowed. "Thanks, Steve," she said softly. 'I'll hang on to that."

They leaned against the ledge, finishing their last sandwiches and watching the sandpipers run on the beach. Perhaps it was time to work again, but they felt too comfortable and lazy to move.

"I hear you've met the Colony gang," Steve said, and Linda grinned.

"They're a swell crew and a bunch of owls," she said cheerfully. "They still got a couple of hours to go after they've met the midnight train in Brunswick to feed lobsters to the engineer."

Steve chuckled, but he shook his head. "I can't keep up with them often. Seven A.M. rolls around too soon."

"I know. I tried it this week," Linda exclaimed. "I'd have to be on vacation to take that pace, and Dad brought me along to paint. He's got to work in Boston next year, but I'm supposed to qualify for Art Students League by the time we get home again."

She studied Steve with frank curiosity. "What about you?" she asked. "Your mother says she's got one coastguardman and one marine architect already. I know you're going to Bowdoin. Then what? Boats?"

Steve's smile was a trifle crooked. "Purchases always build boats or sail 'em," he admitted, "but I can't seem to make up my mind."

7 • The Man On The Beach

BACK on the roof, Steven went to work again mechanically, his mind on Linda's question. "Maybe I'm a drifter," he muttered. He planned to do his hitch of service in the Navy like brother Tom. He did not even have to stop to think about that. But what came later bothered him, and he had to decide soon if he wanted to gear his work at Bowdoin to the future. Neither of his brothers had had any struggle. They both had one-track minds like Linda. Bob was a blue-water man and always would be. The Coast Guard was a natural for him. And Tom still thought anyone who didn't want to build boats had a screw loose. Listening to his plans for expanding the family boat yard, you could take it for granted that Purchas ships would make yachting history yet.

I guess I'm nuts, Steve thought impatiently. He knew that he wanted to stay around salt water and he was bone proud of the work his father turned out. He'd have to settle for the boat yard in the end. Why couldn't he have said so instead of hedging? Neither the Coast Guard nor the Merchant Marine actually made sense for him. Underneath, he knew he was no blue-water man. He liked the Bay where he could drift along the ledges in a

47

skiff watching sand dollars on the bottoms, or stop and explore a tide pool.

The afternoon wore on slowly. Steve felt as if his hands went on prying and tossing almost of their own volition, but down on the ground the piles of old shingles grew impressive. By four-thirty the roof was nearly clear. He wedged himself tight behind the seaward chimney to finish the last patch and tackled it with revived energy. He probably had housemaid's knee, but he'd be through in another fifteen minutes. And right on the nose, too, he thought with satisfaction when he chucked the last broken shingles over the gutter and looked at his watch again. Now all he had to worry about was unlimbering enough to make it down the ladder.

He hooked an arm over the chimney brace for support and stood a minute looking out across the Head. The tide had turned, and a swim before supper would be an idea if he could make Juniper Point in time. He had promised to whistle for Linda before he left, of course, but she had probably grown tired of hanging around long ago. He would see her later anyway; they were all having supper aboard the *Delight*.

Loosing his hold on the chimney rod, he was ready to slide for his ladder when Linda suddenly popped into sight on the beach. The tangled shrubbery in the old Farr graveyard had hidden her before, but now he could see her clearly, running like a rabbit. The Harpswell Harbor side of the Head was all sand and clam flats. Anybody could tear along that. Linda, though, was heading down the Merriconeag shore where the going got worse every minute. Steve was furious. Even a girl born in a city ought to have wits enough not to try to sprint over a beach that could give a mountain goat the jitters. He

48

stuck a couple of fingers in his mouth and whistled frantically.

Obviously Linda heard him. She threw one arm up in acknowledgment, but she didn't slow down. She had been running along the upper level of the shore where the rocks were comparatively small and sand lay between them. Now she began to swerve toward the water. Out there the rocks gave way to boulders and corrugated ledges covered with slippery rockweed.

Somehow, without shooting on over the gutter, Steve managed to skid to the top of his ladder and twist around, his feet feeling automatically for the rungs. He hated to turn his head away from the girl jumping from ledge to ledge on the beach, but he needed his eyes himself. In a minute, though, he was looking shoreward again, and in that minute Linda had slowed down. She was moving almost cautiously, testing each foothold before she trusted her weight on the treacherous weed. Apparently she did have a little sense left after all.

Steve drew a quick breath of relief. But what Linda had seen to make her run that way, he couldn't figure out. Hanging on by one hand, Steve let himself swing as far out from the ladder as he could. He seemed to have a clear enough view; he could even see the lower reaches of the shore, and still there was nothing except the usual kelp and driftwood around. Puzzled, he pulled himself back against the ladder, dropped down another half-dozen rungs, and swung out once more. This time he saw what he had missed before—a group of huge granite boulders above a long line of ledges and at their base, sprawled grotesquely over the weed, the body of a man. For a split second he hung there horrified. Then, as he watched, the figure pushed to its hands and knees and

49

crawled forward a foot or two before it collapsed. Steve's shoulder began to shake with laughter. Oh no, he thought, not that again!

But he sobered quickly. No wonder Linda was running. He had better get down there after her. Maybe he couldn't stop her but at least he could pick up the pieces. He practically slid the rest of the way to the ground and ran across the scrubby field behind the house onto the beach, zigzagging in and out to avoid the bigger rocks and the tangles of weed and driftwood. Ahead of him, Linda's small figure balanced precariously and almost went down. Steve groaned, but, by a miracle, the girl caught herself and jumped safely to another ledge.

Slipping and sliding on the weed, Steve headed diagonally toward the water. He knew that he ought to be watching his own footing more carefully, but he couldn't keep his eyes off Linda. At every jump she made he held his breath. She wasn't used to a rugged shore; her shoes were probably slippery. She made a final spring, and Steve set his teeth. She was teetering wildly. Then she shot out of sight. He tried to redouble his own speed, but it was no good. He still had to pick his way.

Working steadily closer, he strained his ears for the sound of voices. Even if Linda were hurt, he ought to hear something besides the mewing of the gulls and the tide sucking at the litter of shells and pebbles. So far there was nothing. Recklessly, he made a last crazy leap and caught himself against the granite boulders. Somewhere beyond them, Linda's tones blended with a man's deep rumble. Steve climbed gratefully down. It was all right. She was laughing.

But she looked up, contrite, when he appeared. "I heard you whistle so I kept hoping you'd come," she told him. "I just didn't dare wait. Honestly, Steve. First I thought. I saw a dead body on the rocks and then it crawled and I decided someone was hurt. After that, I simply ran."

She looked at the man in the battered dungarees sitting on a rock and began to laugh again. "Oh dear," she gasped, "did you ever see a healthier corpse? Mr. Wood, this is Steve Purchas."

Mr. Wood was feeling apologetic over the excitement he had caused, but he couldn't help smiling. "The first time I met Steve he was exactly the right size to take afternoon naps in a clothesbasket," he said. "Don't tell me you were rushing to my rescue, too, Steve—or were you trying to save Linda's neck? I'm appalled when I realize how easily she might have broken it!"

"It was Linda's neck that was worrying me," Steve admitted. He sat down on a ledge and mopped his hot face. "But I was mad enough to wring it until I spotted you doing that backing and filling stunt of yours, painting."

Mr. Wood nodded ruefully. "I had my paper stretched out on a flat rock. I suppose I do look weird from a distance." His face was distressed. "The Head's been deserted so long it never dawned on me anyone might see the performance and get excited."

"Excited!" Steve said. "I practically had heart failure watching Linda on those ledges. Would you mind hoisting one of those 'men-at-work' signs the next time you try that stunt?"

He pushed to his feet and pulled Linda up alongside him. "If we're going to get back to Juniper Point today, we'd better get started," he told her. "We're not traveling

51

this beach again like a couple of express trains. Are you coming our way, Mr. Wood?"

The man in the dungarees shook his head. "I'll stay a while," he said. "Mrs. Wood is planning to pick me up at the Ash Point road later."

He waved his pipe as Steve and Linda started off together; then he dropped out of sight again behind the boulders.

Picking her way carefully from ledge to ledge, Linda kept unusually silent. She was a bit bruised and shaken up, but that didn't bother her. She was thinking about the man on the beach. She liked these fishing-village people, and the number of things they turned their hands to kept surprising her.

"He's nice, isn't he, Steve?" she said as they neared the Farr graveyard. "Mr. Wood, I mean. Tell me about him, will you? I was scared to death when I slammed around those rocks. I never thought to look at what he was doing. Do you suppose he can really paint?"

Steve stopped so short that she nearly fell over him. "Paint?" he asked in amazement. "Of course, he can paint. Linda Cobb, are you trying to be funny?" He was beginning to look almost as puzzled as she did. "Why, you and Dr. Sutton were talking about him the other day. Naturally, I thought you knew. That man is Orrin Wood!"

Linda shook his arm, incredulous. "Oh no, not Orrin Wood," she whispered. "I thought he was a lobsterman. Steve, what on *earth* would Orrin Wood be doing in a place like this?"

Steve stared at her, his face suddenly shuttered. So he could chalk up another big-town snob for the record after all.

"Orrin Wood was born and brought up in 'a place like

52

this,' " he said evenly. "He went to school with Dad. He always spends the summer here."

8 • Moving day

STEVE retrieved Linda's paintbox from the ledges and fell into step beside her on the path across the Head. He was still tired and hot, and Linda's question had done nothing to cool him under the collar. At least, he knew now what she thought of the place, and, presumably, of its inhabitants. If she wanted to paint from here on in, she could count on getting no interruptions from him. Linda, however, was too well insulated by her own excitement to notice his formal politeness. As long as he answered questions, he could have practiced ventriloquism without making a dent on her for awhile. They had left the Head behind and were well along the Juniper Point road before she even missed the usual easy friendliness in his voice.

But by the time they reached her doorstep she was distinctly annoyed. If Steve thought he could get away with giving her the treatment reserved for snooty tourists, he could think again. She accepted the paintbox he handed her with a "thank you" formal enough to match his manners, but she paused with her foot on the steps to express her opinion.

"If you do happen to know what you're being redheaded about, you might let me in on it someday," she said indignantly. "People always warn you that redhaired men as pigheaded and touchy. I guess I've been lucky not to know any before." Then she sailed on into the house and up the stairs.

She had exactly fifteen minutes to shower and change for Dr. Sutton's supper party, but she made it somehow. The Cobbs were the first aboard the *Delight*. When the Purchases appeared on deck, Linda was still in the middle of her account of the afternoon's excitement. Orrin Wood was well represented in Dr. Sutton's private collection, and his interest matched her own.

"I ought to be embarrassed to tears," Linda admitted. "I made a complete idiot of myself tearing around like a first-aid squad. But all I can think of is that I actually talked to Orrin Wood. *Here!* My goodness, this isn't Provincetown where you fall over people with palettes every six steps. If he had turned out to be Admiral Peary, I wouldn't have batted an eyelash."

Steve could feel his ears getting red. He looked hastily over at Linda, but she was still concentrating on Dr. Sutton.

"I'd have expected a sailor myself," the doctor agreed consolingly. "Artists seem to attract one another. At least, they certainly congregate in the art colonies."

"But Orrin Wood's not our only artist," Mrs. Purchas said. "Elsbeth Rules and Etienne Rienet and Harold Waters are here every summer, too, now, and we already have an art show in August. We don't let anybody forget that."

From then on, Steve decided, the situation got more and more out of hand. He did some unobtrusive maneuvering to corner Linda a minute, but between his father's yarns about Orrin Wood and his mother's tales of art-show personalities, he never got to first base. And at supper, practically the entire length of the table managed

54

somehow to get in his way. Short of strongarm tactics, there was nothing he could do about it at the moment. Just the same, he had no intention of spending the entire night in the doghouse.

This was the *Delight's* last day in Purchas Basin, however, and Dr. Sutton's guests lingered, chatting long after his crew had cleared away the table on the afterdeck. Captain Pel had finished the cruiser's repairs, and tomorrow she would weigh anchor for Harpswell Harbor beside Graveyard Head.

"Waity claims I'll need to pull my shades over there," the doctor said, smiling.

"A bit populous after the Basin," Captain Pel admitted. "Harpswell Harbor's home port for the Merriconeag Yacht Club. Race days are busiest, of course, but you won't get lonesome. Summer young people buzz around there day and night. It keeps the Coast Guard patrol boats nosing in and out with an eye to accidents." He chuckled reminiscently. "Prohibition days, rum-runners avoided *that harbor* like poison."

Steve thought the doctor looked somewhat taken aback by the prospect, but anyone who liked people as much as he did was bound to enjoy that anchorage. His crew, of course, would revel in it. With visiting cruisers putting in nights, there was always plenty of scuttle butt. It was no place to keep a secret.

Dr. Cobb, with a word of apology, looked at his watch and made a reluctant move to leave. "Don't let me disturb the rest of you," he said, "but I've got to run over to Augusta tomorrow and I still have some material to get ready."

"And Pel and I are going to Popham for the day." Mrs. Purchas rose with him, nodding at her family. "It's high time we were all ashore. We hate to have you leave us, though, Doctor. We'll miss you on the Point."

"You won't even have a chance," the doctor warned her cheerfully. "I'll be on·your doorsteps daily, wanting just as much advice as ever."

They all strolled across to the boarding steps together, and Steve did not have to waste energy being subtle. He steered his mother and father firmly into the skiff with Dr. Cobb and stranded Linda in his own. Ignoring him, she turned a little to wave at Dr. Sutton as they headed for the landing, but there was still enough light to see her expression. Steve fixed his eyes on the curls around one ear.

"They're not red," he remarked hopefully. "She probably has a forgiving nature. Besides, I'll sit up and beg if she's got a dog biscuit handy."

Linda laughed in spite of herself. "Not for my dog biscuit, you won't," she retorted. "You're too unpredictable. You might growl the minute you got it."

"Not even a 'woof,'" Steve promised hastily. "I'm just a lap dog at heart!"

Watching the length of leg he was unfurling for a jump to the float, Linda chuckled. She had called him redheaded, and maybe touchy and pigheaded, too. She couldn't remember exactly. But she still didn't know what ·she had said or done to annoy him in the first place. Right now it didn't seem to matter too much. Steve made the skiff fast, and they wandered along the wharf to the path. A young moon hung high in the sky. It was a night made for lingering, and he saw no sense in turning a conveniently narrow path into a race track. He smiled down at the girl close behind him.

"Whatever it was, I didn't mean it, Steve," she exclaimed.

"Next time I'll be brilliant," he assured her. "Just ask me what on earth Orrin Wood would be doing in a place like this and I'll figure you're talking about Admiral Peary. What could be simpler?"

Linda gasped. "Did I say that? No wonder you thought I was an insulting heel. Maybe *I'd* better beg for that dog biscuit!"

She curled both hands appealingly, and Steve marched her to her front door. "You'd better get in there quick," he threatened, grinning. "You're a 'disturbin' woman' and I'm getting as unsettled as Shubael Farr."

Linda tore through her breakfast dishes next morning as if cup handles grew back like crabs' legs. All she had left to worry over was the chicken that Steve's mother had showed her how to fix, and if she cooked that now, she'd only have to reheat it at suppertime. She did not even have to prepare lunch. Her father had already started for his appointment in Augusta, and the rest of the day was hers. Shedding tears furiously, she chopped up onions to add to her bowlful of seasoned bread crumbs and popped the stuffed bird into the oven. Eleven o'clock and you'll be done, she thought with satisfaction. Then she settled down with the Sunday papers.

The chicken was cooked and cooling on the kitchen table, and she was about ready to consider a sandwich for herself when Steven banged at the back door. "Dinner?" he asked hopefully, but Linda promptly squashed that notion.

"Nothing doing," she told him. "That's Dad's supper, and you needn't try to work on my sympathies either. I saw what your mother left you."

Steve looked reproachful. "Hardly more than this and that," he told her. "It could stand supplementing. If they hadn't eloped with the car, we'd go get a spoogie."

"We can have western sandwiches. I saved some onions." Linda hunted in the refrigerator for eggs and ham. "But what under the sun's a spoogie?"

"A nice little Italian sandwich." Steve stirred onions for her enthusiastically. "The roll's a foot long and they stuff it. Onions and cheese and lettuce and meat and peppers and tomatoes doused with olive-oil dressing. I'll buy you one the first time we go to Brunswick to the movies. How about tomorrow night?"

"I'd love it," Linda said.

"Better have some indigestion pills along." Dr. Sutton poked his head around the doorframe. "I've been knocking out there," he explained, "but Steve was so busy itemizing that grocery list he calls a sandwich, nobody heard me." He strolled in and joined them at the kitchen table, eying their westerns with appreciation. "I came to see whether you'd cruise around to the Head with me. I'll bring you back overland in the covered wagon."

The pair of them nodded eagerly. "We'll come if you eat lunch with us," Linda said, laughing. She got out slices of bread and broke more eggs and ham into the rest of the fried onions. "You certainly can't stand being surrounded by us if you don't."

They went out in the *Delight's* tender together and clambered aboard. Standing on deck, chatting with Dr. Sutton, Linda watched the preparations for departure, fascinated. It was an old story to Steve, of course, and he gave the crew a willing hand.

"Waity says all Purchases have salt water instead of blood in their veins," the doctor told Linda. "Anyway, that young man has. I've been watching him from the deck here evenings. He spends hours on the ledges, studying the tide pools and the weed. They're quite a family, Linda, all of them."

The *Delight* began to cut through the blue waters of the Basin, heading for Potts Harbor and the long tip of Harpswell Neck, and the doctor relaxed comfortably beside his guests in a deck chair.

"Moving day's no trouble if it merely means shifting anchor from one harbor to another," he said. "The day's perfect. Let's enjoy it."

"Sailing weather," Steve called it, and he pointed to the sloops dotting the Bay in every direction. The cruiser saluted three or four in friendly fashion, giving them right of way, as she navigated the Gut off the Neck. Then she reached for the Sound, and Linda looked around her, enchanted.

"If a little sloop's so lovely, no wonder people say a clipper was the most beautiful thing man ever created," she exclaimed.

The Merriconeag waters bore a score of sails—big and little—yawls, sloops, ketches, even a catboat or two. Steve studied them interestedly.

"Half a dozen of them laid over after the inter-Bay race yesterday," he explained. "They're on their way home. Look at the designs on the pennants at their mastheads, Linda, if you want to know which ones belong to the same yacht club." He indicated the sloop in the lead. "She's one of Dad's, and that's a Small Pointer a boat's length behind her. They're good all right, but a Purchas-built sloop will show her heels to 'em."

Dr. Sutton gave the Purchas sloop a keen scrutiny, but he obviously reserved his real enthusiasm for motor cruisers. He turned his binoculars with undisguised interest on every one they sighted.

"There are four or five handsome craft nearby," he said finally. "Know any of them, Steve?"

The three of them turned to look astern, and Steve nodded.

"Two of them, sir. One's an Orr's Island boat and another's out of South Freeport. I never saw any of the rest before, but the Bay's always full of visitors in the summer, just cruising or putting in for tuna like that pulpit-rigged gray job farthest out. We get our quota nights in both harbors, Potts and Harpswell."

He watched the sportsmen's ship cut a buoy deliberately and shook his head. "Probably the kind of idiots who don't use their charts either," he said. "Waste of good Coast Guard fuel bothering to go out after them; they're always hanging themselves up on some ledge." Then he chuckled, pointing to the gray patrol boat slipping around the end of the Neck. "They'll get an earful this time anyway. That's the Coast Guard hailing them now."

He dismissed the cruisers indifferently and smiled at Linda. "Let's get a before-and-after look at the Head," he suggested. "Next week you'll be able to see why it got its name. I'm tackling the graveyard Saturday."

"Then it's my last chance to remind you to save the wild things for Loraney," she said promptly. "You coming, too, Doctor?"

Their host shook his head. "Go on and be energetic if you have to," he said lazily. "I'm much too comfortable to move."

He picked up his binoculars again, and the other two made their way forward to settle in the bow where they could watch the features of Graveyard Head take shape.

"Why, it's loveliest when you approach it from the water," Linda exclaimed. "Oh, dear, do you suppose Dr. Sutton is even remembering to look?"

Steve glanced back along the deck. When he craned his neck, he could spot the doctor with the binoculars to his eyes, but they were still obviously trained on the other cruisers. "He doesn't see a thing except those motor ships," he reported, and Linda gave up.

"I guess owning anything as luxurious as the *Delight* is enough to make you motor-minded," she admitted, "but I wouldn't waste five minutes on those cruisers if there was a sail in sight!"

Why anyone would go cruising around on diesels when he could use sails was something Steve had never figured out either, and he nodded vigorous agreement.

"Oh, well," he said, "a man's got to have one quirk just to keep him human, and every other way, Dr. Sutton's the best they come."

9 • *Lights Beyond The Basin*

LINDA hurried the chicken back into the oven as soon as they came home from Graveyard Head. Then she slid into a bathing suit and ran down to the float. Steve was already loafing comfortably in the sun, but he rolled over on his stomach and propped himself on his elbows to watch her buckle her cap under her chin.

"I shoved the icebergs out of your way," he told her,

61

"so you can dive right in. I'll lie here and cheer like crazy."

"That's what you think!" she retorted.

Circling cautiously, she caught him off guard with a neat flank movement, and he hit the water fast. Linda smiled contentedly at his howl of misery, but she planned to be elsewhere before he emerged. Diving hastily overboard, she came up again a safe distance offshore to bob up and down derisively.

"Yow!" Steve raced for the float and hauled up in a hurry. "You'd better stay where you're safe, you doggone polar bear. Just wait till I thaw!"

Linda flipped a scornful hand at him, but she went on avoiding the float. Moving along in a ridiculous duck waddle, she paddled right on by and scrambled out on the beach.

"See you later maybe," she called, grinning, and sprinted for the house.

Steve chuckled and stretched out again for a last toasting. Eight days ago he had been prowling around the Point wondering what the place would be like with summer people underfoot. The answer was easy: cockeyed! Between the Cobbs and Dr. Sutton, he had hardly been off Juniper Point for a week. Maybe, if he could work up enough energy, he'd stick the outboard in a skiff later and chase over to Randall's just to see what was cooking in the town. Reaching for his T-shirt, he finally got to his feet and started up the wharf. His family had probably shown up and he ought to be getting decent for supper, but he was still in no mood to hurry. Down in the Harbor, past Bar Island, three cruisers had already put in and anchored for the night, and Steve stopped to take a look. Even at this distance he recognized two of them as ships

Dr. Sutton had asked about earlier, a big white pleasure yacht and that gray tuna-rigged job the Coast Guard had hailed. She looked like a powerful craft with plenty of speed. Steve shrugged his shoulders as he turned away. Tuna headquarters were across the Sound at Orr's Island. What she'd be doing lying over in Potts Harbor he wouldn't know, but he had given up trying to figure out the vagaries of visiting sportsmen.

There was still no Ford in the barn, he noticed, when he neared the house, but the phone had begun to ring insistently. Steve took the steps two at a time. Ring four —that was Purchas. It was his family at the other end of the line, explaining that they were staying overnight in Popham and that his father wanted him to get a message to Wait Webber.

"There's a quart of corn chowder in the refrigerator, Steve," his mother said, "and an apple pie in the pantry. You won't starve."

"Never have yet," her son assured her. "Don't you begin worrying about me. Tell Dad I'll walk over to Waity's tonight. I'll be seeing you in the morning."

Steve took his time about supper, and the sun was setting before he left the house. He wouldn't make Randall's, but at least it was good walking weather. Often enough he had had to plow over to Ash Point on snowshoes. Telephones were on Waity's black list. Females stuck like barnacles along the lines, he said, eating the nourishment clean out of your words, and he was not aiming to feed them.

Dr. Cobb and Linda, walking up from the beach, whistled at him, and Steve stopped to say hello. "Everything go all right in Augusta, Dr. Cobb?" he asked.

The biologist laughed. "Depends on your point of view,

I guess," he said cheerfully. "That project I undertook seems to have grown. By the way, do you know anything about that staked-out quahog bed I just found on the shore?"

Steve looked at him, surprised. "Why, sure," he said. "It's mine, Dr. Cobb. The canners want to find out whether shellfish farming's feasible on a commerical scale and the Sea and Shore Fisheries people got me started with a couple of bushels of seed clams. The flats here used to be so full of soft-shell clams you could dig a mess in ten minutes; now they're scarcer than hen's teeth. It's not just digging that's to blame, nor pollution either. There's something more. I wish I knew what."

Dr. Cobb nodded. "That makes two of us," he said with satisfaction. "Frankly, I was hoping that quahog bed was yours. I'm afraid I'm going to have to turn you into an apprentice lab assistant, Steve; I need another pair of hands. The canners are subsidizing these experiments I'll be making, and we'll have twenty tanks of young quahogs in the place next week. I'm glad you're interested."

Linda chuckled, remembering Dr. Sutton's remarks aboard the *Delight*.

"You can't scare Steve with a few clams, Dad. He's as bad as you are. Dr. Sutton says he spends his nights hanging around tide pools."

Steve grinned at her. "It's a good thing my brothers aren't here," he admitted. "They wouldn't be half that polite. They always thought I was bats."

He turned back to her father eagerly, and Dr. Cobb explained something of what he was planning.

"I'll be working on a soft-shell disease or two, water-belly, for example, but if you people have to plant qua-

64

hogs to supplement your soft-shells, there's a lot of information still needed. Salinity, type of bottom, temperatures they like—those are the things we'll be experimenting with."

The pair of them grew so absorbed talking controlled temperatures and test plots that Linda finally protested.

"I can feel a shell growing right over me," she said. "About five minutes more with you two and it'll close up tight."

Steve glanced at his watch in astonishment. He had been hanging around talking for an hour and he still had a walk ahead of him.

"How about coming over to Ash Point with me?" he asked Linda. "I've got to leave a message at Wait's for Dad, but I'll even stop and point out Orrin Wood's to you. What more do you want out of life anyway?"

Dr. Cobb leaned back comfortably against his porch railing and watched them start up the path. "Better get that shell rubbed off along the way," he told his daughter, "or we'll be popping you into a quahog tank. Want a flashlight for the trip back, Steve?"

"Got one in my pocket, sir." Steve patted his hip. "Thanks just the same. We'll be seeing you later."

"You mean you'll be hearing me snore," Dr. Cobb corrected him. "I've done too much driving today. I can't keep my eyes open."

He obviously meant it, for the house was dark except for a lamp in the living room when Steve and Linda wandered back at ten-thirty. They had found Waity struggling with a patch in the leg of his dungarees, and Linda had insisted on taking over.

"Something scandalous the way the wind peeks in at me through that hole," he had told them solemnly. "You

65

take a reef in her, Linda, and I'll find us some doughnuts."

But with the tang of salt and pines scenting the air, ten-thirty was much too early to coop yourself up in a house.

"Let's walk down to the tip of the Point," Steve suggested. "You don't want to go in yet, do you?"

Linda shook her head emphatically and they strolled on to the landing. Across Purchas Basin, lights still danced on the water from scattered cottages on the Ash Point shore. But on this side the scrap of moonlight barely dented the darkness, and they could see phosphorescence bright against the pilings of the wharf. Climbing down over the rocks, they took to the beach, stopping to switch on Steve's torch and watch the crabs scurry for the shelter of the rockweed. Then Linda found a tide pool and wanted to hunt for starfish. She would have stayed the rest of the evening if Steve hadn't remembered a bigger pool further along the ledges where he often found sea anemones and he hauled her off to poke in that.

"Oh look, I've found one." Flat on her stomach, Linda was circling the flashlight carefully around the new pool. "Steve, please come get it for me."

She looked up, impatient when he didn't answer, and found him staring intently out over the water beyond the land's end.

"Queer recurring light out there somewhere," he told her. "Turn off the torch and come take a look."

For a minute Linda could see nothing. Then a beam of light cut the darkness, stayed briefly, disappeared, shone bright and steady again, and was gone.

Could it be a flashing buoy?" she asked puzzled, but Steve shook his head.

"There's no buoy out there," he said. "Looks like

lobster thieves. Bije Pinkham has a pound off the Causeway, but it takes gall to operate so close to the Neck road where a light can be spotted. I'm sorry, Linda; I'll have to stick with this. Around here we like lobster thieves just the way cattlemen like rustlers."

"I can understand that," Linda said. "At least there are two of us. What are we supposed to do?"

"First, let them know someone's awake and on his toes," Steve told her. "Have you got that torch handy? We can do a little light-flashing, too. I might throw a scare into them."

"Right." Linda handed over the flashlight and waited for the next move. "You don't think they saw our light before?"

"Not if they're lobster thieves or they'd have stayed dark themselves until they were sure we'd cleared out." Steve began swinging the torch in a wide arc. "There's a skiff tied up to that pine over there." He turned the light on the tree to show her. "Could you get it loose while I dig the oars out? You and I are going for a nice moonlight row!"

It was a feat getting knots out in the dark, but Linda was ready to help shove the skiff into the water when Steve ran back. Then she climbed into the bow and they pulled away from the shore. Steve said nothing for a time, just rowed with that choppy lobsterman's stroke of his, and Linda took her cue from him, thinking he might be trying to map out a campaign. She had noticed it was only his voice he had muffled; he didn't seem to care how far the creaking of the oarlocks carried. When he did speak, though, his sober voice told her what had been worrying him.

"I shouldn't have dragged you into this, Linda," he

admitted. "I'm not looking for real trouble. I still think they'll skip, but if I'm wrong, get down on the bottom of the skiff and put your head under that thwart you're sitting on. Some of these fellows have a mean way with a boat hook."

"Aye, aye, sir!" Linda kept her voice casual. "But don't be so smug about taking the credit for bringing me along. A fat chance you'd have had of getting off without me!"

Steve sounded relieved. "You're okay," he said. "Now, cock your ears, will you? We're going to drift a bit and listen."

He shipped the oars, and they sat quiet again, waiting for some guiding sound. It came soon: the rattle of oars in oarlocks and an almost indistinguishable murmur of voices.

"You got the torch?" Steve whispered.

"No, you have," Linda whispered back.

Steve grunted as he felt hurriedly around the floor boards at his feet. "I must have left it ashore," he muttered. "We'll never see their faces. Oh well, it can't be helped now. Sit tight, Linda; we're going to move fast."

He poked the nose of the skiff into the tide and bent hard to his oars. Then suddenly a beam of light played over his shoulders and he jerked his head around.

"Ahoy, there," he shouted. "What boat's that?"

There was no answer, and Steve rowed furiously. In the bow, Linda sat tense and silent, listening.

"They've turned tail," she cried triumphantly. "You've done it, Steve."

"We've done it, you mean." Steve was panting as he relaxed to listen. "I'm sorry we didn't get a look at them, but they're gone anyway. That's something."

"It's the most important thing for Mr. Pinkham's lobster

pound," Linda said happily, "and they sure are going!"

Steve laughed. The other boat was making no attempt to hide the sounds of its retreat, but Steve and Linda took no chances. They patrolled the area for nearly an hour to be sure the retreat was not a fake before they rowed back to the wharf at Juniper Point.

"We'll find the flashlight in the morning," Steve said, and Linda assented sleepily. It was after one o'clock, and she was ready to call it quits when they reached her front door.

"Let's have an old-fashioned, quiet day for a change tomorrow," she suggested, "not even a body on a beach." Then all of a sudden she chuckled. "The next time Dad wants to settle in a fishing village, I'm going to find out first whether *you* call the place 'respectably dull'!"

10 • *The Unpleasant Mr. Wiggins*

DR. COBB gave Steve time off on Monday morning to report the lobster thieves to Bije Pinkham, and Bije promptly rigged up an alarm on top of his lobster car, noisy enough to fetch the Coast Guard. But nothing could have been more serenely tranquil than Harpswell Township for the next three nights. Then, on Thursday, Captain Nahum Stover's dog raised such a rumpus at midnight that the captain got outside in time to send a charge of buckshot whistling over a skiff in the vicinity of his pound.

Linda brought the news of fresh excitment back to

Juniper Point Friday noon. She had been over to Graveyard Head to paint and had talked to Abby Beamish, still hard at work on Dr. Sutton's house. The Stovers were the closest neighbors to the old Farr place, and Abby had heard the story early.

"So they're trying the east shore now," Steve exclaimed when Linda raced into the lab to tell him about it. "I suppose from their point of view they're running into pretty bad luck—first a pair of dimwits hunting starfish in the middle of the night and then a dog with insomnia. But it's nothing to what they'll run into if some lobsterman gets his hands on them. They'll lie low now for a while, that's sure—unless they have suicidal tendencies!"

Linda grinned at him. "Abby says it beats tarnation how hard a lazy man will heave and shove to turn a dishonest penny."

Steve chuckled. "She's got something there at that," he agreed.

"Well, that's the tale up to date." Linda rescued her paintbox from a chair and started for the door. "I'm off to rustle up a sandwich and get back to work."

"Going to Dr. Sutton's again?" Steve asked, but the girl shook her head.

"Not on your life," she said frankly. "Abby'd have the next installment of the 'Vanishing Lobster Thieves' ready for me and I want to paint. Dad's away for supper so I don't have a thing on my conscience. I can stay at the Causeway all afternoon."

"Then come on down to the Town Landing if you want a ride back," Steve told her. "I'll be over about five to get some stuff at the store."

Linda took him up in a hurry. "I'd already started

feeling sorry for my feet," she admitted. "Just don't forget me or I'll sell you for lobster bait."

But she was still not in sight when Steve had finished his mother's errands at Randall's and stowed the packages aboard the *Maquoit*. Tired of waiting, he finally tramped up the road as far as the brow of the hill and looked across to Pinkham's Beach. Linda was there all right, nonchalantly sitting on a rock, washing a paintbrush in a jar of water. She probably thinks it's still two o'clock, he decided resignedly.

Whistling to attract her attention, Steve trudged over the Causeway and turned onto the grassy path above the shore. There was another artist at work, too, he noticed, but he was in too much of a hurry to get Linda started home to waste more than a glance when he passed. It was nobody he knew anyway—a man with a long horse face and a firm set to his lips.

Linda was dutifully packing her stuff away as Steve reached her. "How come you're so early?" she asked. "Are you playing hooky from work?"

Steve grinned. "Hooky?" he repeated. "Wake up and live, woman; it's five-thirty now."

He stuck his wrist watch under her nose, and they headed back to the road. Linda nodded in the direction of the man just in front of them.

"Did you see my neighbor?" she inquired. "He's been here almost as long as I have."

Impulsively she stopped beside the artist to say hello. "I'm Linda Cobb," she said, smiling. "I meant to come over before, but the light was changing so fast I didn't dare stop working. I hope you've been having good luck."

The man stiffened. Flipping a piece of paper over his

71

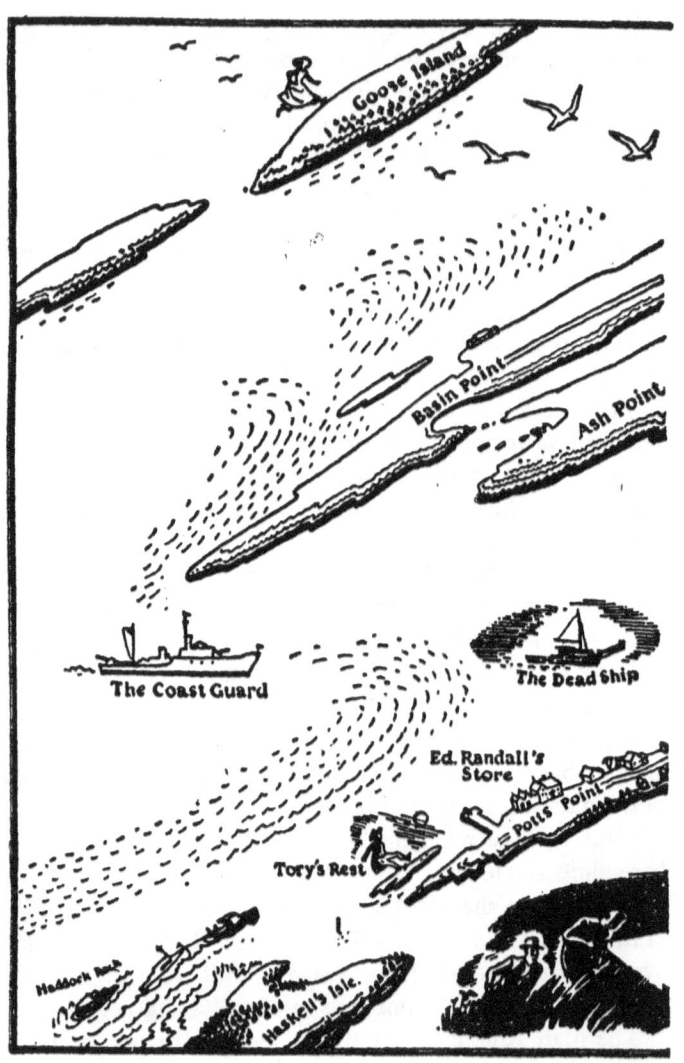

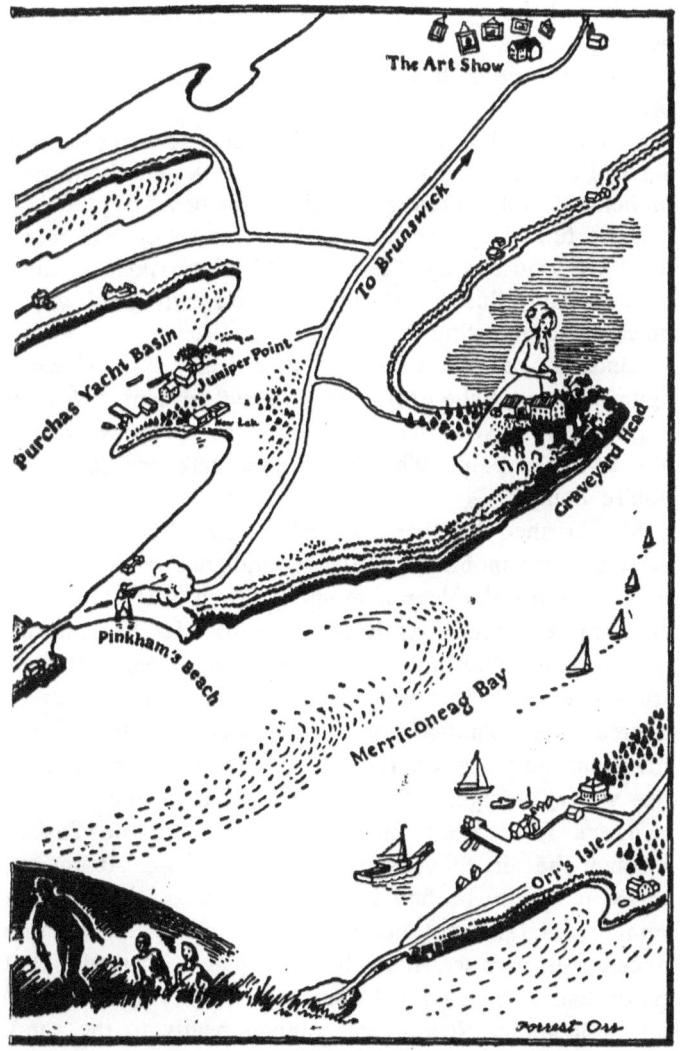

The Art Show

To Brunswick

Purchas Yacht Basin

Juniper Point

Bow Lab.

Graveyard Head

Pinkham's Beach

Merriconeag Bay

Orr's Isle

Forrest Orr

73

sketch pad, he eyed the girl with annoyance written all over his face.

"The afternoon has been quite satisfactory," he said brusquely.

Linda flushed. "I'm sorry if I intruded. It won't happen again, I assure you." Her voice was stony, and she turned on her heel and walked rapidly down the beach.

Steve fumed by her side. "Of all the rotten bad manners!" he said angrily. "I wanted to take a poke at him. He's probably third rate, Linda. Nobody any good would be caught dead acting that way."

Linda looked more stunned than angry. "I just can't figure him out," she exclaimed in bewilderment. "Usually a paintbox in your hand is open-sesame to everybody else trying to paint. They all stop to talk and see what you're doing."

She brushed her hand quickly across her eyes, and Steve's anger mounted. Growling indignantly, he looked back over his shoulder a moment. Their surly acquaintance was apparently ready to leave, too. He had packed up his sketch pad, and that loose sheet of paper he had stuck over it so fast was whipping toward the water at a great rate. Vindictively Steve hoped that it had the man's masterpiece on the other side. It never reached the water, though. With a single smooth motion, the painter's hand went to his belt and a knife flashed through the air. Steve stopped dead, staring. At various times in his life he had watched sailors toss knives with remarkable skill, but he never expected to see a more expert performance than he had just witnessed. That paper had been a good twenty-five feet down the beach and still going. Now it was pinned neatly to the sand,

74

not through the middle where the knife could do damage, but through an upper corner.

Somehow Steve got his feet in motion again. Linda had missed that exhibition and he had no intention of telling her about it, at least not now. Lots of people threw knives for the fun of it; he used to practice on an old pine stump himself. But when anyone so thoroughly disagreeable tossed them that expertly, it was hard to keep your imagination under control. There was no sense in stirring Linda up still more. The dance at the Grange tonight would be a lot more comfortable subject.

"Come on and go with me," he urged. "Waity's calling for square dances. You know you couldn't bear to miss that."

Linda's gamin grin was in evidence again. "I'll say I couldn't," she admitted. "Besides, I've never been to a grange dance. I'll be ready whenever you say."

In fact, to make up for the afternoon, she was actually waiting when Steve banged on the Cobb door at nine o'clock, and they set off contentedly for North Harpswell. Linda had already met two of Steve's high-school crowd; they had double-dated with Bart Merryman and Sally Haskell the night they went to Brunswick to introduce her to spoogies. Now, of course, she met more, but she knew that she couldn't like any of them better than she liked Bart and Sal.

"Sal's the prettiest girl I've ever seen," she said enthusiastically as they danced past the other two.

Steve smiled down at the dark head under his chin. "Sal's all right if you go for willowy blondes," he answered cheerfully. He couldn't see anything wrong with his own lot tonight. That swirly red thing Linda had on suited her fine, and he frankly preferred brown eyes to

75

blue. Maybe she didn't know it, but half the bird dogs in the place had been pointing in her direction ever since she got on the floor. He steered her expertly toward the Coke the minute the music stopped, and stayed on the job. Too many boys he knew were drifting his way with predatory looks on their faces.

But Steve never thought to reckon with Wait Webber. Linda had looked around for him when they first came in. He wasn't in sight, and she had promptly accused Steve of luring her to the dance under false pretenses.

"Deceived, that's what I was," she said mournfully, and Bart Merryman had beamed at her.

"So that's how this Purchas trapped an innocent little city gal again," he remarked with satisfaction. "We knew it wasn't his fatal charm, didn't we, Sal?" He ducked his future roommate's punch and came up grinning. "If you want the horrible truth, Linda, Waity takes to the tall timber far from women every time he quits calling."

"You really mean he never dances at all?" Linda had asked, laughing, and Bart finally backed down.

"Well, maybe not exactly," he admitted, "but he sure makes certain any partner he picks has an extra healthy husband!"

Since Linda obviously did not fit into Bart's category, Steve should have been safe. Waity, however, fixed a thoughtful eye on her from the moment he strolled back into the Grange Hall. Resplendent in black dungarees and red plaid shirt, he put them all through their paces, his own feet shuffling happily on the side lines. Then some way, he was behind Steve. "Swing your partners and back in place," he chanted, and suddenly there was no place for Steve to go back to. Waity was in it, smiling at him blandly.

"Why, you unprincipled old pirate! Next time I'll hold your head under water with my own hands." Steve couldn't help grinning in spite of Bart's and Sal's jeers. "Hereafter you drag your own gal; I'm putting a 'no-trespassing sign' on mine."

Spotting his brother Bob's friend, Seth Green, near the door, he wandered over that way. Sometimes Seth got a letter when the family didn't, and Steve was eager for any news. But by the time he had wormed his way through the dancers, Seth had disappeared outside, and Steve ambled on out alone. The cool air felt good after the crowded Grange Hall, so he strolled on toward the road. Over by the street light, Dr. Sutton was walking away from his Jeepster, and Steve had started forward to hail him when a peremptory voice called, "Just a second, Doctor!"

Steve hesitated. Then, catching sight of a long horse face, he stepped hastily back into the shadows. He had no hankering for a second encounter with the artist Linda and he had run into on Pinkham's Beach. He stayed where he was and hoped that the two would move on. Eavesdropping was not in his plans, but he could hardly help overhearing the conversation.

"Any contact, Dr. Sutton?" the artist demanded in a low voice.

Steve could see the doctor shake his head.

"Not yet, Wiggins," he answered, "though I think they made an attempt last night and muffed it badly. You'll have to have patience."

The pair moved on together, and Steve went back to the dance, that scrap of conversation nagging at his mind. He couldn't help thinking of the episode off Captain Stover's the night before. Maybe they weren't dealing with lobster thieves. The business could be even less pleasant. But how in blazes would Dr. Sutton get involved with an unsavory character like Wiggins?

11 • The "Dead Ship"

STEVE kept that fragment of conversation to himself. After all, it was none of his business to whom Dr. Sutton talked, and he was too busy to worry about it often, for now that the tanks of young quahogs had arrived Dr. Cobb had turned their care over to him. What he had learned to do, he knew, was simple enough, but he had a man-sized job on his hands revamping his high-school laboratory techniques to suit his new instructor's exacting requirements. Though he was grateful for every hour he had spent over a microscope or a test tube, he realized that he was learning more in a week of this kind of individual supervision than he could have learned in a month of ordinary classroom work. When he was helping Dr. Cobb handle a Petri dish with a culture-growing dab of agar in it, he would hardly have missed the rest of Juniper Point if it had slid into the Bay. Nothing he had ever encountered before was as interesting as this biological warfare on shellfish diseases. This was work that he loved.

"My goodness, baby-sitting," Linda said gleefully when she poked her head in one morning and found him changing water and charting temperatures.

Steve looked around to smile at her, and the smudge

of paint on the end of her nose reminded him of the afternoon on the Causeway. If Linda had happened to be painting on Graveyard Head, she might have told Dr. Sutton about her encounter with "Horse Face" and learned something about him.

"Ever seen that man we met on Pinkham's Beach again?" he asked.

Linda made a wry face. "I'll say I have," she said disgustedly. "He acts as if he owns the Head. Dad and I even saw him wandering down the path the other night when we went over to look at the new wallpaper. Dr. Sutton seems pretty vague about him, but you know what a lamb the doctor is. He thinks he ought to encourage any artist, even a blot on the landscape like that one. I'm painting right here the rest of the week. That man hardens my arteries."

Steve, without really seeing her, watched her wander off to hunt for her father. That episode outside the Grange had suddenly begun to trouble him again. He could easily believe Dr. Sutton was vague about Wiggins. Everybody knew the doctor was a pushover for artists. He took them at face value without asking inconvenient questions, and Wiggins could be banking on that. The longer he thought about it, the less Steve liked it.

As soon as he cleaned up his work at the lab, he began to look for Linda. He had decided to tell her the whole story. Maybe she could get a clue as to what Wiggins had up his sleeve. Wandering around with her paintbox, she got to know everything that went on in Harpswell. She was naturally friendly, and people stopped so often to watch her paint that she came home as full of news as the *Brunswick Record*.

79

Right now, he discovered, she had even managed to pick up an audience on Juniper Point. A skiff was pulled up on the beach, and she was talking eagerly to a man sitting crosslegged on the sand beside her. For a second, Steve slowed down; then he recognized Orrin Wood and went striding ahead. He had no intention of telling anyone except Linda about that conversation he had overheard, but this might be a chance for information. Ten to one, Mr. Wood himself had encountered Wiggins somewhere. Maybe he knew the man's reputation as an artist.

The pair on the sand glanced up at the sound of footsteps, and Steve chuckled to himself. Linda looked as if a fairy godmother had just handed her a passport to Paradise.

"Hi, Steve," she said. "I've been watching Mr. Wood paint."

The artist smiled. "She spotted a body on the beach again, but this time she took my antics in her stride. Why didn't one of you tell me that Linda painted?"

"She's good, isn't she, Mr. Wood?" Steve asked.

Linda gasped in horror, but Mr. Wood did not seem to mind being pinned down.

"She is," he said decisively. "I've been explaining the art show coming up. I'd like to see her put something on exhibit."

"Why not?" Steve grinned down at Linda's dazed face. "At least she can't complain the artists she meets on Juniper Point are anything like the one on Pinkham's Beach."

"A longfaced individual carved out of an iceberg?" the artist asked, curious.

"His name's Wiggins," Steve volunteered. "I found that much out."

"So did I," Orrin Wood admitted. "I asked Ed Randall about him after a slightly surprising encounter yesterday morning on the Head, but Ed didn't know much more than his name—just that he's rented a cottage on Hurricane Ridge. I'm reasonably sure he's not a professional. Perhaps he's one of these sensitive amateurs with an inferiority complex."

Steve snorted. "If you mean his manners are inferior, you're dead right, and I wouldn't trust him near my woodpile either."

Orrin Wood shoved his skiff into the water and climbed aboard. "I'll let you know if I learn anything more. And don't forget that art show, Linda. There's a Bay-history and legend classification this year if that gives you any ideas."

Steve and Linda watched him off and started back to the Cobbs', talking earnestly. Between the art show and Wiggins they had considerable ground to cover. But Steve's story of the conversation outside the Grange drove Linda's excitement over the show temporarily out of her head.

"Those remarks about a contact and a muffed attempt could mean that the skiff Capatin Stover sighted didn't belong to lobster thieves, couldn't it?" she asked thoughtfully. "Maybe the one we sighted didn't either."

Steve nodded. "Smuggling ought to be more in Wiggins's line. He's no piker; lobsters would be too piddling for him. I don't care how soon he sticks his own neck out for the Coast Guard, but apparently he's trying to use Dr. Sutton for a fall guy. You'll have to keep your eyes and ears open, Linda. I'm stuck here on the Point most of the time."

"Back I go to the Head," Linda agreed. "Just seeing me around annoys him. That's some satisfaction!"

But she got no chance to paint anywhere the next day. Steve shanghaied her for company when Dr. Cobb sent him to Portland for a consignment of laboratory supplies, and they left soon after breakfast to make a day of it.

The morning went fine. Steve stowed Dr. Cobb's packages securely away on the *Maquoit,* and he and Linda did the town. It would have been smooth sailing all day, they decided afterward, if they had just omitted the movies. But they went unconcernedly to the first show, and when they came out again, ready to start home, fog was drifting through the city streets. Down at the water front, the Bay had already been blotted out.

Steve could have kicked himself. Fog frightened a lot of people, and they were in for a slow, cold, wet two hours of it on the water. Of course, Linda had been along when they struggled through pea soup after the *Delight,* but that had been different on two counts: they had had their hands full every minute, and his father had been in command. She seemed cheerful as a cricket, however. Bundled up in a slicker out of the *Maquoit's* cabin, she settled companionably in the cockpit to take care of their foghorn, blasting away at regular intervals.

"Oh listen!" She smiled at him as Portland Head Light wailed its warning. "I've found us a beautiful echo."

"I get you into something every time we're together," Steve said apologetically, "but at least you can trust the *Maquoit.* She'll find her way home alone."

"If you think I'm worrying, forget it." Linda's tone was serene. "The day I start getting scared on the water I won't have a Purchas for skipper."

Her smile was so confident that Steve's heart did a

nose dive before he came up with a smile again. He had navigated Casco Bay in every kind of weather; he was not actually worrying. Just the same, he did not like fog. It meant strain and tension—and accidents happened. Now, with Linda on his hands, he had no desire whatever to play Robinson Crusoe all night on some weed-covered ledge. He settled down resolutely to the business of getting his ship and his passenger safely back to port.

"Keep that horn in action," he warned Linda as the *Maquoit* nosed her cautious way through harbor traffic and out into the Bay.

After that, the going grew more and more monotonous. Pine-studded islands slipped invisibly past their bow, and the pound of blue water creaming white against fog-shrouded cliffs reached their ears queerly distorted. Nearly an hour went by in slow motion. Then the muted throb of a ship's engines and the blast of her foghorn warned them the Casco Bay Line's *Aucocisco* was making her own slow return trip from the islands to Portland. Linda's answering blasts roared throatily across the water, and the *Aucocisco* acknowledged them promptly. Still they saw nothing though they wallowed in her wash. But somewhere in the distance a wharf bell began to toll, and Steve peered at his compass.

"That's Long Island guiding her in," he said with satisfaction. "We're not doing too badly ourselves. We'll run for Chebeague and then the channel between Little Bang and Stockman. When you hear the bell buoy, we won't be far from home."

Linda smiled at him, but she was shivering a little, and Steve pulled her into the circle of his arm, wrapping his own slicker over her knees in spite of her energetic protests.

83

"Arguing with the skipper constitutes mutiny aboard this ship," he said. "Besides, why'd I need a slicker with a nice warm windbreak like you handy?"

Linda wrinkled her nose at him, but she settled back against his shoulder, contentedly humming snatches of "Pinafore" between the howls of their horn.

"I've always wondered whether people could sleep through foghorns," she said after a while. She closed her eyes experimentally. "My goodness, it'd be no trouble at all!"

"Here, none of that," Steve protested. He bent his head quickly and kissed her hard.

Linda sat up in a hurry, her eyes wide open, but he pulled her back against his shoulder.

"Don't go away," he said severly. "It's in the regulations. Captain's duty. Discipline for people who fall asleep on watch."

So kissing her came under the head of disciplinary duty, did it! Linda tilted her face up to his, looking angelic.

"Why, of course," she agreed. "Exactly like having to stay aboard your sinking ship."

Her expression could hardly have been more demure, but Steve's eyes glinted.

"I keep forgetting you're a landlubber," he exclaimed. "Now pay attention. There's a subtle difference. I'll have to kiss you again so you'll get the idea."

He leaned over, but Linda was ducking for the horn. "I think I heard a boat out there somewhere," she said. "We'd better keep this going."

Steve shook his head in disapproval. "You interrupted the lesson," he said reproachfully, "and you can't

84

spend your summers in Harpswell without understanding these things. Remind me to take it up later."

"Naturally! I'll make a note of it on my calendar the minute we get in." Linda laughed at him from the security of her new perch, and Steve chuckled.

"You'll be cold again over there by yourself," he pointed out. "Come on back. I'll keep the skipper under control."

"No tricks?" she demanded.

"No tricks," he said.

He held out a persuasive hand, and Linda slipped hers into it, settling back beside him under the slicker. He seemed to forget to let go, but she didn't pull away. The fog isolated them in a microscopic world. Linda's left hand stayed on the horn, but there were no answering wails—nothing except the lonely reverberations of their own blasts, and the pressure of his fingers on hers was warm and comforting. She looked up at him, and his hand closed tighter over hers.

"You're so easy to like," he said unexpectedly.

The teasing note had left his voice, and Linda felt suddenly content.

I can't find too much wrong with the skipper either," she admitted and liked the way his mouth curved when he smiled.

Steve kept the *Maquoit* steadily on her course. "Listen," he said. "Hear that bell bouy? Half an hour more and you'll be eating doughnuts in your own kitchen."

He glanced at the *Maquoit's* compass. All was well, and apparently they had the Bay to themselves. Lobstermen would have been in a long ago, and the summer sailors would have headed for harbor when the fog first began to roll across the islands. Steve began to watch the compass again, getting ready to work their way around Horse Island.

There was not much more than the harbor left to worry him now. Then Linda's frightened gasp and a frantic blast from their own foghorn jerked him into attention. Looming beside them in the fog, so close that he could have reached out and touched her with his hand, was the gray hull of a ship.

He swerved the *Maquoit* safely to port, bellowing indignantly. "Ahoy, you to starboard! Are you asleep up there? Where's your foghorn?"

But the only answer he got was the muffled echo of his own shout against the fog. Then the gray shape disappeared.

Linda had been watching wide eyed. "The Flying Dutchman," she whispered.

A queer expression flickered over Steve's grim face. "The 'Dead Ship' " he muttered under his breath. Then he caught himself. "Blasted pirates," he said angrily.

But Linda would not let him get away with it. "Come on, give," she ordered. "What's the 'Dead Ship'?"

"Nothing but a legend," Steve told her. "It just popped into my head when you said 'Flying Dutchman,' that's all"

"You mean this Bay's supposed to have a ghost ship and you never even bothered to tell me?" Linda demanded accusingly. "All right, pal; you can start talking now! What's her name?"

"Never heard any," Steve said. "She's just the 'Dead Ship of Harpswell' as far as I know Nobody at her helm; nobody on her decks. Grandfather said she's supposed to come in all sails set and drawing even in a calm, but she never reaches port, just drifts out to sea again.

Whittier wrote a poem about her. Mom used to read it to us when we were kids.

"*Let young eyes watch from neck and point,*
And sea-worn elders pray—
The ghost of what was once a ship
Is sailing up the bay."

Linda's face lighted up eagerly. "Lend it to me, will you, Steve? My education's been neglected."

Steve nodded. It was all right with him if Linda wanted to moon over the old legend. All he wanted was to see that the Coast Guard got hold of men reckless enough to risk people's lives in a fog that way. He was still furious when he finally moored the *Maquoit* and rowed Linda in to Purchas Landing. Unloading the lab supplies would have to wait over till the next day, but reporting that incident was not going to wait any longer than it would take for him to reach the telephone.

12 • Tory's Rest

STEVE was out on the *Maquoit* next morning tossing the lab stuff he had left aboard her into his skiff when a coast guard buoy tender slowed down alongside.

"Thought you might like to know somebody else saw that gray hull yesterday," the helmsman called. "A lobsterman phoned in mad as a wet hen, but some old codger with him kept butting in on the call insisting the 'Dead Ship' was cruising again!"

Steve quit work and leaned over the *Maquoit's* rail

to answer. "My passenger called her the 'Flying Dutchman,'" he said, shrugging, "but, if you ask me, a Coast Guard cutter would have given that ghost plenty of trouble. Her hull looked substantial enough to scare the daylights out of me; I could practically see myself going down for the third time. Thanks for keeping me posted."

He waved at the retreating buoy tender and threw the last cartons into the skiff.

"That 'Dead Ship' yarn'll be all over the Bay by suppertime," he muttered as he rowed back to Purchas Landing. "Next thing, there'll be a ghost epidemic."

He made a mental note to tell Linda the coastguardman's tale. She had blown into their kitchen last night while he and his father were still discussing the grayhull incident, but she had been a lot more interested in the "Dead Ship" legend than she was in her escape from being rammed. She had pumped his father for every old wives' tale he could remember about the phantom, borrowed his mother's copy of Whittier, and blown out again, looking as if someone had just deeded her a gold mine instead of coming within an ace of drowning her. Steve had not seen her since, but he suspected that she had gone across to the Head this morning to paint. Wiggins, he knew, was likely to find her perched casually in any of his haunts. He might not enjoy Linda's proximity, but he had no monopoly on the scenery. She had been painting up and down the shore now for a good four weeks, and everybody knew it, including Wiggins. He had run into her often enough, first off the Causeway and then on the Head, and if he had a cottage on the Ridge, he must have had to duck to miss her there.

But once inside the lab, Steve shoved both Linda and the "Dead Ship" out of his mind. Some diggers had

88

brought in a half dozen baskets of softshell clams, packed up in wet weed the way Dr. Cobb had wanted them, and the place was littered. He tended to his young quahogs in a rush and pitched into cleaning up the mess on the floor. They were working under enough handicaps in a quarter-finished building without slipping and breaking a leg. Most of the stuff was rockweed, but he found odds and ends of devil's apron and Irish moss and agar weed and ribbon kelp, even a few pieces of that papery crimson weed he'd seen anchored to rocky bottoms below low-tide mark. He had never happened to handle it before and he was still studying the bright red strands when Dr. Cobb came along.

"Grinnellia," the biologist said, nodding at the specimen in Steves hand. "Ever hear of English laver? It's gathered by the seacoast people and boiled and eaten like a vegetable. Porphyra is its scientific name. This Grinnellia you've got is a close relative in-looks though it's very much smaller."

"I still think I'll use mine for fertilizer," Steve said, grinning, "though I've got to admit I like the puddings they harvest this sea moss for. Over at Lowell's Cove where they weigh in, a couple of the men told me a raker with gumption can earn himself about thirty dollars a day mossing two tides. At one and a half cents a pound, that adds up to an awful lot of pudding!"

. Dr. Cobb chuckled. "Don't bother working up an appetite," he advised. "All that moss won't turn into pudding. A lot of it will end up sizing cloth and curing leather. I've eaten candied kelp stalks out in California, but most American kelps are harvested commercially for making the algin that manufacturers use in cosmetics, medicines, ice cream, and chocolate milk."

He leaned over and picked up a piece of the purplish-brown agar weed. "This is the stuff in my Petri dishes." he said. "It makes the culture material that we grow bacteria in. The New England varieties are small, but on the Pacific Coast Gelidium gets as long as five feet."

Steve listened attentively. This was the kind of thing he wanted to know more about. But for a second, his brother's accusing voice came echoing again out of the past.

"Good night, Grandfather, he didn't catch anything! He wasn't fishing. He was just poking in some weed on a ledge. That's all he ever wants to do."

Even now, Steve could almost see his grandfather's eyes crinkle up as he considered Bob's indictment.

"Just poking, eh?" he'd asked interestedly. "Well, good can come of poking, Bob. The Bay's got a lot to teach a boy, and there's more than one way to like salt water."

Steve gratefully remembered his grandfather's defense as he went back to tidying up. He knew that he had always felt secretly guilty when he failed to conform to the family pattern. But working with Dr. Cobb was giving him a fresh slant on things now. If his mind was still poking in seaweed, did it make sense to drift into a boat-yard job just because his family happened to build boats? He loved sailing and he loved boats, but maybe it was time to stop trying to kid himself into believing that he wanted to make a career out of either of them. If his way of liking salt water wasn't Bob's way or Tom's either, at least this summer had taught him he need not apologize for it. Someday, between the biologists and the biochemists, wringing a decent living from the sea might be a less rugged business. Why not face it for once and

90

admit that he would rather help accomplish that than send fifty trophy winners down the ways?

By noon, when he finally carted the seaweed home for fertilizer, Steve was in a sober state of mind. It was easy to tell himself he wanted to spend the rest of his life on marine biology, but he wasn't the only person involved. What about his family? His father didn't actually need him in the boat yard; he'd have Tom. But this decision meant more than the question of another pair of hands in the yard; it meant the possibility of letting his family down. No Purchas had ever let another down yet, and that was one family pattern Steve had no intention of tearing. What he needed, he decided, was some of the "settin' and thinkin' " his grandfather used to recommend. Somehow he had to work out a way to convince his father that a Purchas in a marine biological laboratory was as logical as a Purchas on a ship or in a boat yard. If he could manage that, everybody would be satisfied.

He dumped the weed on his mother's compost heap and strolled on into the house. Mr. Wood had stopped by, hunting for Linda, and was staying for dinner with them. Rumors of the "Dead Ship's" appearance were already buzzing up and down Ash Point, and the artist was curious to hear the facts behind the sudden revival of interest in the old tale.

"Lots of men are mean enough to risk the other fellow's neck without giving a hand," Captain Pel said after Steve had told the story, "but the meaner they are, the more unlikely they'll risk their own necks, too—unless there's money in it. That's what makes me suspicious of a ship plowing through a fog like yesterday's without a horn. The whole business puts me in mind again of the

91

Prohibition rumrunners, Orrin. Most of those fellows had the ethics of a shark."

Mr. Wood nodded. "Unsavory," he agreed. "Just the same, you can tell Linda for me that she's been lucky; she's picked up a subject for a Harpswell legend picture firsthand."

The Purchases looked at one another and laughed. "I guess we don't need to," Steve explained. "She was in here last night squeezing Dad dry on details. We knew she was up to something."

Captain Pel smiled. "I went to bed feeling like a lemon rind," he said. "Linda certainly acted as if those tarnation pirates had done her a personal favor nearly ramming my boat. You can tell her something for me, too: this picture had better be good!"

It was after seven-thirty, however, before Steve had a chance to hunt up Linda. Then he found her investigating the Cobbs' empty breadbox.

"I knew it!" she exclaimed. "I heard Dad stirring around down here. He's swiped every bit of bread in the house to feed that one-legged sea gull he found. Just as if he didn't know the dratted thing would rather have a tasty snack of garbage! Now, what'll I do? He went off with the car."

Steve laughed at her disgusted expression. "We'll put the outboard in a skiff and zoom over to Randall's. But hurry up if you're coming, will you? It looks like rain."

Linda grabbed her pea jacket off a hook, and they dashed down to the float together. It did look like rain. The wind was blowing southeast, and dark clouds were scuttling across the last rose streaks of the sunset. Steve opened the outboard's throttle wide.

"By the way, I painted nearly all day on the Head,"

Linda called over the noise, "but that Wiggins man wasn't in sight. I met Abby, though, when I was leaving, so at least I know why." She chuckled, remembering, and Steve grinned at her.

Okay," he said, "let's have it. Did they meet head on?"

Linda nodded. "I'll say they did! Apparently Abby caught him snooping around the house and took off after him like a heavy bomber. I got the impression he'd prefer painting some other scenery for a while. I'll try the Ridge next."

"Go to it," Steve said approvingly. "Now, I'd better bring you up to date, too." He gave her the coastguardman's report and told her Orrin Wood had been looking for her. "He wanted to suggest the 'Dead Ship' for your Harpswell-legend painting."

"It'd be a good one for him," Linda confessed; "fog's his specialty. I've been struggling with that 'Dead Ship' all day on the Head and the fog keeps getting me down. Never mind; I'll get it yet!"

Looking at the determined set of her chin, Steve smiled to himself. He waved his arm at the island-studded bay. "Three hundred and sixty-five islands and a ghost on every one of 'em. Just help yourself if the 'Dead Ship' goes sour."

But Linda's chin stayed set. "It isn't going sour," she said subbornly as they tied up at the Town Landing.

It was dark when they finally drifted out of Randall's Store. They had run into Bart Merryman and Sally Haskell, and the four of them had hung around to talk awhile and drink Cokes. Besides, with everybody in the place demanding an account of their "Dead Ship" experience, they were lucky to get away at all.

"I never felt so important before in my life," Linda exclaimed after they got outside. "Someone should have tried to sink me sooner!"

She and Sally wandered down the wharf together, leaving Bart and Steve to trail behind.

"Those two get along," Bart said comfortably. "Sal says double dates have picked up since you've been bringing Linda."

The girls were still talking when they caught up with them on the float, and Steve steadied the skiff. "Hop in by Linda, Sal," he suggested. "We'll drop the pair of you off at Bart's float." He grinned at his friend. "Taxi, mister?"

The chugged off past the Casco Bay Line wharf toward the end of Potts Point. The weather was still being cooperative, but the clouds were as threatening as ever, and they didn't linger at Merryman's. "See you," Steve said briefly, and swung the skiff out for the trip back. Seated in the stern, he kept his eyes ahead, intent on giving a wide berth to half a dozen lobster boats and sloops moored offshore. Linda, facing him amidships, gazed around her, carefree.

"The moon's breaking through,' she said. "I guess we'll get home dry."

Steve glanced up. The moon had shaken herself free of clouds and was cutting a silver path through the water, drenching reefs and islands in a sudden white light, He knew it would not last long; the clouds were too heavy, but they might as well enjoy it for a minute. He hand reached forward to shut off the motor; then he yanked it hastily back. Someone was marooned on a ledge out there.

Linda spotted the figure at the same moment. "Turn

94

around, Steve; please, quick." Her voice rose in excitement. "Somebody's stuck on the rocks!"

Steve raced the skiff back. The moonlight had faded as fast as it had appeared. In the darkness, they couldn't even see the ledge any more, let alone a figure on it.

"Never mind," Steve said reassuringly. "Maybe he can't see us, but he can certainly hear us coming. Quit worrying, Linda. We'll pick him up all right."

He shut off the outboard and nosed the skiff cautiously in toward the rocks. "Be right with you," he shouted cheerfully.

Then they drifted gently against the side of the ledge, and Linda stared in puzzled bewilderment. "Why, there's nobody here," she said as Steve began lighting a series of matches, "nobody at all."

"Hold the skiff still a minute, will you, Linda?" Steve asked, and climbed over to scour the rocks. Weed covered the lower reaches of the ledge, but there was plenty of dry, firm surface. No one, unless he did it deliberately, could possibly slip off.

"We can't both have been seeing things," Steve insisted. "There must have been somebody here." He was starting to get back in the skiff when his shoe touched something that cracked, and he bent over quickly to pick it up. "Feels like a pack of cigarettes," he said. Then he dropped down on the thwart beside Linda and tossed it into her lap. "Hang on to it, will you, while I strike a match?"

It was a pack of cigarettes all right, half full and quite fresh. From the dry, clean state of its cellophane wrapping, it could not have been on the ledge more than a short time.

Linda drew a long breath of relief. "Thank goodness,"

she said fervently. "I was beginning to think we'd both gone nuts!"

Steve muttered agreement absent-mindedly. He was busy trying to figure out what had happened on the ledge.

"If you swim decently, you can make shore from Tory's Rest—so that's what this man must have done," he told her. "Only, why'd he go diving into ice water as soon as he heard us coming? Doggone it, Linda, it's crazy."

13 • *Wait Webber's Story*

THE first drops of rain began to spatter down, and Steve shrugged resignedly. "We're in for it now. I know our disappearing friend hasn't done anything to rate it, but I hate to leave till we're sure he made shore."

For answer, Linda turned up the collar of her pea jacket and settled in the bottom of the skiff. "Go right ahead," she said calmly. "But if you spot him, just let me know. I'm saving up a couple of questions I'd like to ask."

They had no flashlight, but for twenty minutes they prowled the waters off Potts Point as conscientiously and as thoroughly as they could, even cutting off the motor once in a while to listen for a swimmer's splash or a cry for help. They they gave up and turned back toward Purchas Landing, completely drenched and completely disgusted.

"I only hope he's more waterlogged than we are," Linda said vehemently. "Next time anybody gets marooned on a reef, remind me to look the other way." She stayed silent a minute thinking the situation over; then she came out with a question. "What did you say the name of that ledge was?"

"Tory's Rest," Steve told her, "and if that pack of cigarettes hadn't spoiled everything, by tomorrow we could have set up in a new business: Cobb and Purchas, Practicing Mediums!" He was laughing at himself, but Linda knew that he was worried. She could hear the strained note in his voice. "First we raised the "Dead Ship' and then we raised the Tory. Great guns, we *had* to be psychic."

"Is he another legend?" Linda inquired. "Because if he is, you can tell me about him and take my mind off the puddle I'm sitting in." She was still huddled against Steve's knees trying to persuade herself that the side of the skiff offered some shelter, but her imagination wasn't good enough. "Anyway, if I help scare up a ghost, I ought to be properly introduced to him."

"The Tory's history," Steve told her. "At least, the facts are true. The story dates back to the Revolution when the British had already burned Portland to ashes. After that, Bay people didn't play ball with anyone who wore the king's colors, and every time a British frigate showed up, they made a dive for their guns. By then, they'd got in the habit of shooting first and asking questions second, and this lobsterback didn't have any more sense than to drop over the side of a frigate and swim ashore. Maybe he really was deserting, but the Harpswell men didn't wait to find out. Besides, they'd caught sight of his face and recognized him for a Loyalist. He had to take to the water again, and a bullet got him when he was resting on that ledge. It's been Tory's Rest ever since."

"Well, after tonight, he's welcome to it," Linda said feelingly, "but if we ever get dry again, would you be willing to sit down and put an 'X marks the spot' on every ghost walk on the chart of this Bay? I think I've got an idea."

She did not elaborate, but at that point ideas meant nothing in Steve's life unless they involved hot showers and dry clothes. He was busy getting everything he could out of the outboard, and once back on Juniper Point he made a dash with Linda for the Cobbs' house and a fireplace. Dr. Cobb was home again, and Dr. Sutton had only just dropped in, bringing the Purchases with him. They were talking over plans for a house-warming on Graveyard Head. All four of them looked up in amazement as Steve and Linda tore in the door.

"My stars!" Deborah Purchas was aghast. "What have you two been up to?"

She started to hurry her son home for a bath and fresh clothes, but Dr. Sutton disapproved.

"Hot showers and rubdowns for both of them right now," he ordered. "Let Alex root out a bathrobe for Steve while you're making some hot cocoa. And hurry back and give an account of yourselves," he called as Steve and Linda ran for the stairs.

The group around the fire was all frankly curious when Steve rejoined them, but he refused to do any talking until Linda pattered down the stairs a little later, a chart of the Bay tucked under her arm. Then toasting comfortably on the .floor in front of the fire,

together they told their story between sips of hot chocolate.

"Don't ask us what that man was doing on Tory's
Rest," Steve said finally. "We only know he was there
one minute and gone the next." He pulled the pack of
cigarettes out of his pocket and tossed it on his father's
lap. "These were bone dry and fresh when we found
them on the ledge. They hadn't been on that weed more
than a few seconds."

Captain Pel eyed the pack thoughtfully before he
dropped it back in his son's hand. "You two did the only
thing you could do under the circumstances," he said
with approval. "You certainly couldn't pull away without
making sure no one was in real trouble." He began to
smile. "Waity saw a couple of college boys from the
Ridge racing each other to Brunswick on foot the other
night. They hadn't covered much more than six miles
by the time he came back." The captain chuckled. "I'd
swim to Tory's Rest myself in preference. Maybe your
vanishing Tory was another bet settler."

The pair on the floor stared at each other blankly; then
Steve nodded. "Could be," he admitted, grinning. "At
least, it makes some kind of sense, and that's more than
anything else does."

"Sensible nonsense, anyway," Dr. Sutton said cheerfully. He relaxed in his chair again, looking relieved that
one of them had wits enough to come up with a possible
explanation, and watched Linda spread the chart on the
floor. "Trying to find Tory's Rest?" he asked.

"Not just that," she explained eagerly. "I want to
draw a 'Ghost Map' for the art show. It ought to be fun.
Would you all help me?"

Mrs. Purchas promptly shoved her knitting aside and

99

dropped down on the floor. "Why didn't somebody think of that before?" she demanded. "Visitors will love it!" She put her finger on Harpswell Neck. "You can start with our ghosts, Linda. You know them already."

"Don't forget that girl that's supposed to run across Goose, or the Spaniard at the bottom of Ghost Cliff over on Ragged." Captain Pel had found an old envelope in his pocket and had started listing ghosts systematically. "And there's the white moss with the blood on it and the haunted cellar at Chebeague."

"How about old Kieff on Cliff Island?" Steve asked. "Wasn't he the beauty who showed false lights so ships would pile up on the reefs and he'd get fat on the salvage?"

Linda's pencil scurried frantically over her chart as their suggestions mounted, and Captain Pel's eyes twinkled. He leaned down and began to count the islands she had marked, shaking his head disparagingly. "Barely scratched the surface yet," he said. "You hunt up Waity tomorrow, Linda. His mother had a half brother who lived with them after he retired from sea. The old man was a spiritualist, and Waity got spoonfed on what his Uncle Jed called 'manifestation' in the Bay. He's exactly the man you need."

Knowing Waity, Linda was prepared for salty comments. but not for the sharp look he gave her when she waylaid him next morning outside the boat shop and told him Captain Pel had said that he could tell her about ghosts.

"How'd Captain Peletiah come to say that?" he demanded. "Who's he been listening to over at the store this morning? Ike Trufant?"

Steve, trundling a load of lab rubbish past them on his

100

way to the dump, stopped and grinned. "What's eating you anyway?"

"Ghosts," Waity said disgustedly. "Ike Trufant knows about it. I was visitin' him last night when that storm got ready to come up so I hi'sted sail for home. Dropped my car keys first off, though, and had a time finding them. Had to get out my torch and hunt through a patch of blueberries. That's how I happened to notice."

"Notice what?" Steve asked impatiently. Ike Trufant's place was well down Potts Point, about in line with Tory's Rest. Maybe Waity knew what had been going on last night. Apparently he had seen something or somebody, but you couldn't hurry Waity. He told things his way.

"That's what I'm trying to tell you, aren't I?" he asked. "By thunder, it was a fellow trying to crawl up out of the water. It shook me up considerable. Course I raised a yell that fetched Ike, and we climbed down on the beach fast as we could. But you know what it's like. Time we'd fetched up against a few outcroppings of ledge, we'd slowed down some and when we struck the reefs, the fellow had disappeared. Ike claims he never was there; says I was seein' things."

"He was there all right," Steve said positively. "Linda and I spotted him standing on Tory's Rest and went tearing out to pick him up. We thought he needed help, but he ducked us, too."

"Did he look like a college student?" Linda asked eagerly. "Captain Pel and Dr. Sutton thought he might be a Bowdoin boy settling a bet."

Waity snorted. "Looked like nothing but a drowned rat." he said. "Dr. Sutton should have been with me instead of parking up on the Ridge. I saw that Jeepster of his when I went past."

"But didn't you hunt for him?" Linda persisted. "He couldn't just have evaporated."

"Certain, we hunted for him," Waity retorted. "Wore my torch out doin' it. Can't think what he did unless he slipped back in the water till we gave up—and why he'd do that beats me." Waity rumbled indignation. "Ike's settin' back laughin'; keeps saying I'm my Uncle Jed's nephew! Just as if I didn't have business of my own to mind without taking off across a beach after a Tory that's been dead a hundred and seventy-five years."

14 • Art Show

ALL the rest of the day, Juniper Point got versions of the Tory yarn on the installment plan. The milkman left a couple with the "grade A," and anyone who ran an errand on the Neck came back with another. By five o'clock, when Steve finally got a chance to stroll into Linda's kitchen, he was ready with advice.

"If you want to hang up some sticky flypaper," he suggested, "the air's buzzing with ghosts you could catch for that map. I've run into a dozen I'd never heard of before."

But Linda brushed the map aside. "Steve, can that man Wiggins be back of this 'funny business'?"

"Maybe not back of it, but mixed up in it somehow," Steve said. "I just bumped into him at the store, making a headache of himself over his grocery list. Ed said he'd been fussing around for the last half-hour; nothing in the place suited him. Personally, I'd like to bet that he was doing some concentrated listening!"

Linda looked at him inquiringly, and Steve shrugged. "I may be crazy, but until somebody gives me a better idea, I'll figure Wiggins is tied in with that ship we met horsing around in the fog. Maybe he wanted to know whether the 'Dead Ship' and the Tory had taken people's minds off lobster thieves for a change. I think he's getting ready for action. He couldn't do much prowling near shore in a boat at night when a bunch of lobstermen thought somebody was after their pounds."

"I wish Wiggins was," Linda admitted. "At least, lobsters couldn't possibly involve Dr. Sutton. I suppose you noticed Waity said he'd seen the Jeepster parked on the Ridge. And the doctor never even mentioned being near Potts Point when we told him about the Tory. If Wiggins would only do something sane just once, waiting for the next move wouldn't be so bad! Right now I keep feeling I belong in a psychopathic ward."

Naturally, the whole township was agog over the way their half-forgotten ghosts had invaded the present. Down at Randall's there were not enough cracker barrels to go around as skeptics and believers battled it out, and Waity, to his infinite disgust, discovered that he had suddenly inherited the mantle of his late Uncle Jed. But there was nothing he could do about it. He was appealed to as an authority by both sides.

"Livelier than Judgment Day," Ed said drily, listening to the talk swirling over his groceries. "The place is full of resurrected ancestors who fell foul of a ghost."

In all the excitement, the art show might have come

103

off a bad second if the enterprising members of the Garden Club, which sponsored it, had not made capital of their history-and-legend theme. With legends jumping out of the pages of books to perform on the ledges and waters of the Bay, nobody wanted to miss pictures about them. Even people who normally ignored art in favor of fishing or sailing began to look forward to the show. In self defense, Waity spread the news of Linda's "Ghost Map," and she promptly came in for a large share of the attention he was more than willing to do without. Local historians dug up apparitions for her as avidly as if they were spading out pirate gold.

Linda was nearly in despair. Official "hanging day" when a committee hung the exhibit entries in the old Meetinghouse at Harpswell Center, was only one more week off, and she was sure that she would never get the map done in time.

"How can you finish something that grows like Jack's beanstalk?" she asked Steve. "Why, I've got six ghosts now for every one I had when I started."

Eventually, of course, she holed up in her own room morning after morning and began to get results. She had already finished the "Dead Ship" and had hidden it away. She had no intention of letting Steve see that until it was hanging on a wall of the Meetinghouse. If he liked it, she meant to give it to him, just as a reminder that all these crazy things did not happen in a dream, and she was not going to present him with a chance to be conventionally polite on the subject. She wanted to catch his expression off guard at the art show. But the "Ghost Map" was different. All the Purchases, and Waity, too, had helped to find original material for her, and she felt as if it belonged partly to them. She was glad when they dropped by to see her progress.

Mrs. Purchas began to worry about Linda after a few \days. "That child will turn into a ghost herself if she doesn't stop long enough to eat decent meals," she told Steve indignantly. "Maybe we'd better have the Cobbs here for suppers."

But her son shook his head. With Orrin Wood around, that art show meant a lot to Linda, and he knew it. He was not letting his mother harry her into sociability. "Forget the suppers," he said, grinning, "but I'll stuff her with doughnuts and sandwiches if any should happen to be lying around about ten o'clock nights."

His mother laughed. "See that you do then, young man," she warned him. "Because I'm not frying dough-nuts just for the pleasure of letting the seams out of all your pants!"

Steve obeyed orders. He had offered to make the frame for the "Ghost Map" and he was working nights in the boatshop, cutting, sanding, and rubbing down the wood under Linda's supervision.

Their conversation inevitably drifted around to Wig-gins some time in the evening, and they spent hours try-ing to fit together the pieces of puzzle. Dr. Sutton was a collector. That was one cue piece. And Wiggins claimed to be an artist. Probably that was another. But where did the lobster-thief alarms, the conversation out-side the Grange, the "Dead Ship," and the Tory belong in the finished picture? There had to be a common denominator somewhere even if they couldn't find it. But, just trying, Steve always managed to work up enough appetite to persuade Linda to help him raid the Purchas kitchen.

"He certainly throws energy around," Bart complained

one night when he and Sal dropped in at the boatshop for a minute. "It's not natural. That guy's been playing the field straight through high school, Linda, but this is the first time he's tied up with a girl who could make him work." He grinned at Steve and hustled Sally toward the door. "Come on, Sal. We're leaving before you start getting ideas."

Steve chuckled as he snapped out the lights. "What a woman! Even my best friends run." He caught Linda's hand and pulled her after him. "All right, slave driver, let's struggle over and sit on your front steps with these sandwiches before I collapse."

"My heart bleeds for you," Linda assured him cheerfully, "but if you can wait till I find my handkerchief, I'll burst into tears."

Steve settled his long legs comfortably and drew Linda down beside him. "Listen," he said. "Music with our meal." Aboard a sloop out in the Basin someone was strumming a guitar, and gay voices floated up to them singing. Linda watched the reflection of the boat's riding lights bob in the water.

"It must be satisfying to take pieces of wood and shape them into something as full of life and personality as a sloop. As much fun as sailing it afterward. No wonder it's hard to make up your mind, Steve; I don't think I could ever really choose."

"Maybe that's why I've picked something different."

His voice was so low that Linda just heard him, and she turned in surprise.

"It's marine biology," he admitted. "Oh, I know it's my life and I've got to live it, but how the heck do I break that to Dad?"

"You mean without hurting him, don't you?" Linda

106

asked. "That's a tough one, Steve. I wish I knew the answer. But I know you can't turn yourself into a shipbuilder if you want to be a biologist. You'd go crazy."

"I'd probably be a rotten shipwright," Steve said ruefully. "Maybe I'll be a rotten biologist, for that matter, but I want a crack at it. Dad's never hog-tied any of us, Linda. He's not that kind. Thats why this has got to make sense to him, too."

"I know that," Linda agreed soberly. "You'll have to keep working on it, that's all. Only isn't it ridiculous! We sit here stewing over Captain Pel, and my father would be rooting for biology."

But the fact that neither of them found any easy solution did not prevent their planning ahead. Psychological warfare, Steve called it finally. It was the night before official "hanging day" and he was fitting her "Ghost Map" into its frame.

"Just make a note to send me a wheel chair the same day I get my doctorate," he said when he stopped to admire her job. "Four years of college, a stretch in the Navy, and graduate work! At least, you're on the way, Linda. You've proved it."

"With one map and a handful of water colors?" she demanded. "When you've worked every day in that lab with Dad? You'd better save *me* the bigger half of that wheel chair, Steve. I'm at the beginning, too!"

"Thanks for saying that, Linda." His eyes held hers gratefully. "Especially when you come up with something like this."

He looked down at the map again, chuckling over the trees showing through the coattails of a ghostly sea captain, and Linda laughed.

"If that Tory ever manages to suit Wait Webber, I'll

think I've achieved something myself," she admitted.

Steve smiled at her. "Don't worry; he will! All that map needs now is sound effects. A little sithering and moaning, and it's guaranteed to stand your hair on end."

Linda held tight to his enthusiasm for the next two days to bolster her courage. She knew that there would be other amateur stuff in the show, but she had never exhibited anything before, except at school, and she went on being nervous until she walked in the door of the old Meetinghouse with Steve and her father. Then she was caught up in the fun and excitement of opening day.

Mrs. Purchas, on hand ahead of them to serve as a hostess, was distributing lists of paintings and artists, and they made their way over to her table.

"Don't forget to vote," she reminded them. "Our visitors are the judges at the Harpswell show. Put the number of the painting you choose on one of those pieces of paper," she waved her hand toward a table by the door, "and drop it in the ballot box when you go out."

Linda glanced around eagerly as they started their tour. "I never dreamed there'd be so many people," she exclaimed. "Where on earth do they come from, Steve?"

"Half over the state," he told her. "Mom says this show has worked up a reputation. It hung Wood and Rienet and Waters from the beginning because all those men summer here, and I guess that attracted attention. Even collectors and dealers from out of the state turn up these days."

"There's one collector here now anyway." Linda pointed out Dr. Sutton in the crowd. "Let's go say hello to him a minute."

But before they could squeeze themselves through the

groups of people blocking their way, the doctor was deep in conversation with a man in yachting clothes beside him, and they hesitated to interrupt.

When they came in, Linda had meant to keep one eye firmly on Steve until after he saw her "Dead Ship," but she kept losing track of him. In the end, while she was busy with a Rienet canvas, he vanished completely, and she had to start on a hunt. Captain Pel had arrived, she discovered. He and her father were standing in front of a table full of ship models. Steve was not with them, however, and Linda drifted on toward the stairway.

She still hadn't seen any of the pictures upstairs. In fact, she suddenly realized, she hadn't seen any of the history-and-legend group, not even her own two. They must be the ones on the stair walls and in the balcony.

Excited and eager, she looked at the printed list in her hand. Why, this might be the most interesting part of the show. The classification included an Elsbeth Rules, a Waters, and two Woods. Inching her way through the people on the stairway, Linda hunted for the paintings that she particularly wanted to see. The Rules, of course, was charming: Harpswell's famous old parson-author, Elijah Kellogg, in his buggy outside his Five-Mile Church, a flame of autumn colors in the trees along the road. And beyond that, the Waters hung, dark and thunderous, its tragic heroine the little schooner *Helen Eliza,* Longfellow's *Hesperus,* fighting an implacable sea.

Now I'll find the Woods soon, Linda thought contentedly as she rounded the curve in the stairs. Then she heard Steve's voice and quickened her step. He was standing above her on the balcony talking to somebody she knew she had seen before. She peered again. Of course, she had seen him. He was the man in yachting clothes who had chatted with Dr. Sutton downstairs. This time, though, she was not letting him scare her off. Determinedly she climbed to the top step, only to be halted by the sound of her own name.

"Miss Cobb is around here somewhere if you want to look," Steve was saying, "but you can see for yourself that the picture is not for sale."

He pointed to a line in the printed sheet in his hand, and the man nodded. "I saw that," he said impatiently, "but I still want to speak to Miss Cobb. Money talks nowadays."

Linda could feel her face grow hot with excitement. It was thrilling to have somebody want to buy one of her pictures even if she was not going to sell it. Hers were both marked N.F.S. because the hanging committee insisted on an indication, not because she had dreamed anyone would want one. At least, she would not feel badly about disappointing this buyer; that cocksure, money-talks tone of his had rubbed her the wrong way.

Steve looked around and saw her nearing them. "Here's Miss Cobb now," he told his companion. "This gentleman wants to talk to you about buying the 'Dead Ship,' Linda. He seems to like it almost as well as I do."

Linda smiled at both of them. "It's pleasant to know that anybody likes it well enough to buy it," she admitted happily, "but it's not for sale. I'm sorry if that's a disappointment."

"Oh come, Miss Cobb," the man sounded faintly condescending. "Let's not close the door quite so fast. I'm prepared to offer a good price. You may be a novice but you're going places someday. Shall we say a hundred dollars?"

Linda did her best to suppress her gasp. This man was either completely crazy or stupid enough to want to get his own way at any cost. She shook her head uncomfortably. "I'm sorry. I can only repeat that the 'Dead Ship' is not for sale."

The man bowed. "I feel you may regret your decision. In that event, my offer will stand for another day." Taking a card from his wallet, he put it in Linda's hand. "I'm anchored in Lowell's Cove for the present," he said casually. "My boat's the *Shark*, rigged for tuna." He bowed again and went rapidly down the stairs.

Steve shook his head. "That guy wants what he wants when he wants it!" he said.

Linda was frowning at the bit of cardboard in her hand. "His name's Max Roberts, but it doesn't mean anything to me—except that he hates to take 'no' for an answer. He made me want to hump my back like a cat!"

Steve smiled at her. "Phew, I feel better!" he admitted. "I was afraid you'd start repenting. That man didn't rate the 'Dead Ship', Linda. Underneath, he doesn't give a hoot for a picture. He's just a gambler who knows a good deal when he sees it, and the 'Dead Ship' is the best thing you've done."

Linda smiled back at him, her eyes shining. "Phew, I feel better," she quoted impudently. "You can wrestle with Mr. Roberts after this. I meant the 'Dead Ship' for you all along if you wanted it."

Steve started to protest. "Not on your life!" he began vigorously. Then he broke off in consternation at the hurt in Linda's face. "Please don't look like that," he begged miserably. "Of course I want it; you painted it. I just can't take it, that's all!"

They were still arguing when Orrin Wood appeared at the top of the stairs and raised a quizzical eyebrow. "I feel like the Irishman in the old chestnut," he said good-naturedly. "Is this a private fight or can anyone get in it?"

"*You* can get in it," Steve said promptly. "Linda turns down a cool hundred dollars for the 'Dead Ship' and then wants to give it to me! Maybe you can make her see sense."

"Mr. Wood knows perfectly well it isn't worth a tenth of that," Linda retorted. "You're just being red-headed again, Steve."

The artist's keen eyes went from one face to the other. "Maybe you'd better start at the beginning," he suggested. "I've got lost along the way."

Steve and Linda looked at each other. "You start," the girl said. "Mr. Roberts tackled you first." Then, while Orrin Wood listened, they managed between them to straighten the story out.

"And even if I had wanted to sell the 'Dead Ship,' how could I take all that money when I know it's worth about ten dollars?" Linda ended indignantly.

Mr. Wood smiled. "Mr. Roberts made it clear it was worth one hundred dollars to him," he pointed out reasonably. "If his offer seems extravagant to you or me, that only means we see the 'Dead Ship' through our eyes, not through his." He swung around to the water color again. "You've handled those grays with imagination," he said, studying the wet mist on the face of the sea and the smokier shadows in a patched plank on the "Dead Ship's" hull. He nodded approvingly from the "Ghost Map" back to the "Dead Ship." "Imagination and humor make an effective combination, Linda, and

112

both pictures have it." Then he began to laugh as he bent over to examine the belligerent masculine figure springing to its feet in the stern of the water-color Maquoit.

"Naturally I wouldn't presume to advise you, Steve, about accepting Linda's gift, but if the lady had given my disposition dead away in paint like that, I'd get that picture into my clutches fast."

Steve tried to look injured. "It's libel," he protested, "and I ought to sue for damages. But I'm so peace loving I suppose I'll just give in as usual." He stopped to grin at Linda's derisive snort. "You can tell Mr. Roberts for me that he's permanently out of luck."

Linda smiled at him. "Now maybe I'd better go look at the rest of these pictures before you can change your well-known peace-loving mind!"

She started to dart off down the balcony, but Steve caught hold of her arm and led her in the opposite direction.

"Don't look now," he said cheerfully. "Your artistic friend Wiggins was standing right behind us. You nearly fell over his feet."

15 • *Ensign Robert Purchas OF The Yakatak*

WEDNESDAY was not the only day Mr. Wiggins visited the art show. Linda reported that she saw him strolling unsociably around on Thursday, and when Steve wandered in late Friday afternoon, just before

113

the show was due to close, he found him planted in front of the "Dead Ship" staring as if he were trying to find a flaw in every brush stroke.

"That guy doesn't do my blood pressure any good," Steve muttered to himself as he watched him finally leave the building.

Mr. Wiggins was almost the last visitor to go. The show was officially over for another season, and the afternoon's hostess tactfully eased out the few lingering stragglers. But by the time Steve had helped his mother lock up and give the keys to the hanging committee so that they could return the pictures to their owners the next morning, it was well past six. Linda had waited outside for them in the Cobbs' station wagon, however, and they drove off together.

Of course, no one knew the results of the balloting yet, but Linda was enthusiastically certain that Orrin Wood's "Graveyard Head" had won.

"There wasn't a thing in the place that could touch his early-morning lights in the water," Linda said. "No wonder Dr. Sutton bought it like a flash. Why, even that Wiggins man acted almost human when he saw it!"

Mrs. Purchas smiled at her. "Are you glad you went into the show yourself, Linda?" The girl nodded.

"It's not just that I learned a lot either," she said thoughtfully. "It was being part of it. All of a sudden I discovered I belonged, almost like a 'native daughter.'"

Contentedly she sent the station wagon purring up over the hill toward the Juniper Point turnoff where the Bay shone cobalt ahead of them in the sunlight. "What's that big ship coming in?" she asked idly.

"Coast guard cutter!" Both Purchases leaned forward eagerly, and Linda stepped harder on the gas.

114

"Do you think it's really your brother's ship out there?" she asked Steve.

"Well, no use our blowing a gasket until we get the glasses on her," he admitted. "But if a cutter in these waters isn't the *Coos Bay*, she's pretty sure to be the *Yakatak*. There's just about a fifty-fifty chance."

Linda pushed the station wagon as fast as she dared to over the twisting Point road, and Steve was practically halfway out, starting for the binoculars, the minute they reached the Purchas steps. But Captain Pel was ahead of him. He came striding up from the landing, the glasses under his arm, and a broad smile on his face. "It's the *Yakatak*, Deborah," he said, and passed the binoculars to his wife and son.

Linda dashed off to her own house almost as excited as the Purchases. She had heard so much about Bob that she felt as if she would recognize him on sight.

"Captain Pel says that cutter carries about ten officers and one hundred twenty enlisted men," she told her father at supper. "Her skipper's a three-striper—commander to you!"

Dr. Cobb nodded. "She's probably in the 311-foot class," he said. "Had the Purchases got wind of young Bob's coming, or is this a surprise?"

"Surprise," Linda told him, "and if he doesn't get shore leave soon, they'll burst."

She had hardly finished up in the kitchen, though, before a tall young man in uniform strode past the house and turned in toward the Purchases' front path. So he's here, she thought with satisfaction as she settled down in the living room to write a letter. This is one night the Purchases don't need company. But the last page of her letter was still ahead of her when Steve

115

came racing in to bring the Cobbs back home with him. Their protests that this should be family night only made him laugh, and Linda found herself unexpectedly smiling at Ensign Robert Purchas on his own hearthstone. He was not hard to like, either, she discovered. He had his mother's laughing eyes and his father's slow, friendly smile, plus a quiet air of command that sat as easily as his uniform on his broad shoulders. She studied the brothers critically as they stood side by side. With those blond waves and that uniform, Bob might have stepped out of a recruiting poster, but even dungareed and redheaded, Steve was exactly as good looking. The two of them were comparing notes about skippering Purchas boats, and Linda dimpled. The *Maquoit*, she decided, had not lost a thing by the change to the redheaded skipper, especially if the crew happened to fall asleep on watch.

"Is the *Yakatak* assigned to the Bay a while?" Dr. Cobb asked interestedly. "She's the first cutter I've happened to see around this summer.

"Our stay's indefinite right now, sir," Bob said, "but the assignment's no secret." He nodded toward the evening papers still lying unread on the table. "There's a news story tonight about some art treasures stolen from Germany. The military traced them to France, and the Sureté managed to follow the trail as far as Marseilles. When they lost it at the water front, they cabled warnings right and left. The stuff hasn't turned up anywhere yet, but there's a general feeling it's headed for the U.S.A. More money here, I guess. Anyway, the Coast Guard's been on the alert all along the Atlantic Coast."

Steve made a dive for the paper. "It's front-page

116

news," he exclaimed. "With illustrations. I never saw either of these pictures before. One of them's not even on canvas. What do you call the painting done on plaster walls, Linda?"

"Frescoes. You paint them on while the wall's still wet." Linda was peering eagerly over his shoulder. "The picture's Spanish, the "Olive Pickers" by Murillo, but I'm not sure about the fresco. It looks Italian though. What's the paper say?"

Steve's eyes raced down the page. "It's Italian all right. Great guns! It was dug up at Pompeii! Of course, the thief had to lug it off, frame and all, but he slashed the Murillo canvas out. The police think he hid in the museum at closing time. Anyway, the stuff disappeared in the night. Didn't somebody try a stunt like this on the 'Mona Lisa' once?"

"Then at least this fellow showed a little more sense," Bob remarked. "Toting the 'Mona Lisa' around with you would be about as handy as toting the Statue of Liberty. Everybody recognizes it."

"This doesn't sound a bit more sensible to me," Mrs. Purchas protested. "A fresco outside a museum is unusual enough to make anyone remember it if he got a glimpse. Besides, I can't see how this thief hopes to dispose of either of these paintings. Museum collections are always being reproduced in books or magazines, and dealers and collectors would recognize these instantly. They certainly couldn't think they were copies with the papers making all this fuss."

"They're hot potatoes all right, Mother," Bob agreed. "Just the same, there are always dishonest dealers, and the FBI people claim some men stop at nothing to add

117

to their collections even if they're scrupulous about everything else."

"I suppose so," Mrs. Purchas admitted. "You know what Waity said when he saw Sereny Atkins chasing after charm-string buttons: 'The beatinest thing about collectin' was the way it begat the gets'!"

Steve could feel his heart thud uncomfortably. A lot of crazy happenings were turning unpleasantly sane. Shooting a glance at Linda, he caught the consternation she was trying to hide and gestured toward the door. "Doggone it, I'm hungry again," he said. "How's for helping me fix some cheese sandwiches? Dad and Bob are always ready to eat."

Neither of them said a word until they were out of earshot in the kitchen on the other side of the house. Then Linda burst out defiantly.

"I don't believe it, Steve! Mr. Wood says Dr. Sutton's the squarest collector in the country. You know yourself he never takes advantage of anybody. He simply couldn't be mixed up in something as dishonest as this."

But there was sick dismay in her eyes. Unwillingly she was listening again to the doctor's voice that first night on Graveyard Head: "I'd do a lot more than outbid a museum to get those two Woods into my possession!"

"I don't want to believe it either," Steve said. "The trouble is it makes sense. It explains Dr. Sutton's interest in visiting boats the day we first saw the lobster thieves and that contact Wiggins asked him about."

"Then why is the Coast Guard just getting on the job?" Linda demanded. "Those things happened weeks ago."

Steve shook his head reluctantly. "I thought of that, too, but it doesn't help any. Bob didn't say the Coast Guard was just getting on the job—only the *Yakatak*.

118

The patrol boats have been around; you've seen them yourself. Cutters often spell Trouble."

"You mean you think they've got wind of something, don't you?" she asked unhappily, and Steve nodded.

"The story breaks in the papers and a cutter carrying a five-inch gun arrives the same day. What can I think?" He banged a clenched fist angrily against the refrigerator. "I'd like to get my hands on Wiggins's neck," he growled. "I told you he might be getting ready for action. Nobody'll ever make me believe a man like Dr. Sutton got mixed up in this of his own accord. Great guns, Linda, the housewarming on Graveyard Head comes off tomorrow. What an unholy mess!"

16 • Housewarming

WHEN Linda parked the station wagon and hurried into the Purchases' Saturday morning, the kitchen looked like a bakeshop. Mrs. Purchas had been on the job since five, and her chairs and tables were loaded with boxes of brownies and pastry tarts and trays of frosted cupcakes. The *Delight's* cook had rolled and checkerboarded sandwiches to store in his refrigerator most of the afternoon before, but Deborah Purchas was taking care of everything else herself. Doughnuts were still ahead of her, and she did not mind a bit. This housewarming was important. She could not remember when anything had given her as much satisfaction as watching the old Farr house come back to life.

119

"Deliveryman," Linda sang out, and Mrs. Purchas looked up to smile at her.

"All these boxes are ready to go," she said briskly. "You're a dear to take them, Linda; I wouldn't trust Steve with a box of brownies as far as I could see him!"

Watching the anticipation in her eyes, Linda nearly lost the smile that she had so carefully pasted on her own face. She could not bear it if anything happened to spoil this party for Steve's mother. Mrs. Purchas had worked nearly as hard as Dr. Sutton to rehabilitate the old garrison house on Graveyard Head. Hour after hour she had helped choose paints and wallpapers and rugs and upholstery, and showed painters just how to match the colors.

"If you'll start loading, I'll finish putting wax paper on these cupcakes," Mrs. Purchas suggested, and Linda nodded quickly.

She was anxious to get away before she spoiled anything herself, glooming around. Ever since she got up she had been trying to believe that nothing unpleasant could possibly happen today, not so soon after the cutter's arrival, but right now she felt as if the *Yakatak* had anchored on her shoulders instead of out in Potts Harbor where it belonged.

At least it was a relief not to see Mr. Wiggins wandering around with his paintbox when she left the cartons of food at the Head. Apparently Abby really had scared him off for a while, and he certainly would not dare to show up this afternoon with a lot of company in sight. Dr. Sutton had had to make a last-minute trip to Brunswick; so he was not there either, and Linda drove down the road again in a more cheerful state of mind. If you had never been good enough to get even a walk-on part in a school play, it was better to start acting in a big room full of people than face to face with the person for whom you were trying to put on the show.

She swung the car right on the Neck road and headed for Harpswell Center. She had to stop and pick up her two pictures from the Meetinghouse, and time was running out. It was nearly twelve, and the hanging-committee people would be leaving.

Linda got in just under the wire. Orrin Wood and Harold Waters were still on duty, and a few exhibitors were carrying out their canvases, but obviously she was the last-comer.

"Your pictures are over there against the wall, Linda," Mr. Wood told her as she panted in. Then he collected his own pictures and went out to stow them in his car. But Linda was waiting for him when he came back to lock up.

"I'm sorry to delay you," she said apologetically. "I looked everywhere I could think of and I can't seem to find the 'Dead Ship.'"

"Why, Harold Waters had your pictures over there with his own stuff. I saw him carry them both downstairs. Wait a minute, Linda; we'll catch him. He's still outside."

Mr. Wood turned and strode hastily to the door. "Harold," he shouted, "what happened to Miss Cobb's 'Dead Ship'? Do you know?"

Mr. Waters poked his head out of his car. "It's in there," he called, "over against the wall where I had my things and the Rienet canvases."

But when Mr. Wood shook his head, he climbed out and came back to investigate. "The map was against the wall and the 'Dead Ship' infront of it," he said, looking puzzled. Then suddenly his face cleared. "Rienet has it, of course; that's what happened. He had a couple of his

121

own things there for a minute and he picked it up with them. I'll stop by right away and get it for you, Miss Cobb."

Linda protested vigorously. "Oh please don't bother," she begged. "It's my own fault for being so late anyway. Mr. Rienet lives on Basin Point, doesn't he? I can run around there on my way home."

She changed her mind, however, after she got back in the station wagon and took time to look at her watch. It was already one o'clock. She was not worrying about her father's lunch; she had fixed coffee and sandwiches for him before she left. But she still had to snatch a bite herself and get the doughnuts over to the Head for Mrs. Purchas. That was not going to leave her any too much time to chase home again and dress. Besides, Mr. Rienet would be at Dr. Sutton's, and it would be more sensible to arrange to go over some time tomorrow when he was sure to be home. Considering all the arguing she had had to do, she imagined Steve would survive one more day without the "Dead Ship."

She routed Steve and her father out of the lab as early as she could, but Captain and Mrs. Purchas drove past her window on their way to Graveyard Head nearly an hour before the other three Juniper Pointers were ready. "Unfashionably late," Dr. Cobb said when they arrived and found the party in full swing. The big house was crowded with people strolling from room to room, exclaiming in delight over the carved jade and ivory that Farr clippers had carried home a hundred years before, and admiring the Chinese rugs and wallpapers that Mrs. Purchas had matched so exactingly to the originals.

Steve's hand tighted on Linda's when he saw her eyes searching apprehensively for Dr. Sutton. "Relax," he or-

122

dered. "Nothing unpleasant seems to be brewing. And we can't get within a mile of Dr. Sutton yet. Let's follow the crowd a while."

They wandered upstairs after the others, but Linda paused a minute when they came down again to smile at Loraney in her golden frame.

"I know she loves having the house come to life around her," she remarked contentedly, "and oh, Steve, I hope your mother is hearing just half the comments people are making. She's responsible for so much of all this beauty."

The groups around Dr. Sutton were thinning, and they began to work their way across the living room. "Of course, I'd never dare mention it to Waity," Linda admitted, laughing, "but Abby Beamish really is a miracle woman. Just look at the mahogany and rosewood in this room! Who'd ever have thought that furniture could look like this again? It positively dazzles your eyes."

They managed to greet their host eventually and wandered on again, hunting for Sally and Bart. Steve had seen them in the distance a few minutes before, but they proved to be elusive.

"Listen," he said finally as they strolled through the back hall. "That's Sal's giggle. They're out on the kitchen porch, the heels." He opened the door and they ducked through. "Waity, too, Linda. Parked next to the source of supplies. Wouldn't you know?"

. The three on the steps grinned at them cheerfully. "Sit right down," Bart said heartily. "Kick off your shoes and take down your hair. Grab yourselves a fistful of brownies. This is 'refugee hall'; a fat lady tramped on Sal's instep."

The newcomers sat down willingly. Sal was still rubbing her foot, but as long as her nylons had come out intact, she was pretty sure she'd survive. Linda's conscience, though, finally made her look at her watch. It was nearly six, and although the chatter and laughter inside sounded as gay as ever, they ought to be getting back before the party ended.

"How's your foot feel, Sal?" Linda was beginning, when Steve suddenly sprang to his feet.

"Do you hear that, Waity?" he interrupted sharply. "That's fire!" Then he was running down the step and across the grass, the rest of them racing after him, Sal's foot forgotten.

Ahead of them wide ribbons of flame were rolling out of Dr. Sutton's rubbish pit, winding over the matting of grass and pine needles, wrapping around a stand of pine and birch; and up Merriconeag Sound, rising dangerously, the wind blew steadily toward the house. Steve stopped their headlong rush. Linda and Sal stood there chilled with horror, but Steve gave them no time to lament.

"Get back to the house, you two," he ordered. "Sal, you phone the fire department; Linda, you find Dr. Sutton and Dad." Then he was running again, yelling to Waity and Bart over his shoulder. "We've got to get Dr. Sutton's crew out of that kitchen; they know where everything is." But two of the crew were already pelting down the path from the back door. "Spotted the fire from the window," they called. "The cook's trying to rouse the fire warden. He'll be along in a minute."

"Axes and shovels, Dave," Steve shouted. "Where are they? We can stop this thing if we hurry."

Without a word, the crewmen swerved aside for the barn, the other three at their heels. It seemed to Steve that they must be moving like snails. In reality, it was only minutes before they had torn back across the grass and started their fight at the pit, Waity and Steve, axes in hand, swinging methodically at two blazing trees; Bart and the crewmen digging desperately at a trench.

Up at the house, Dr. Sutton's guests were streaming out, their hands clutching pitchers and buckets and saucepans, whatever they had been able to grab.

"Tide's high," Captain Pel roared. "Get down to the shore, everybody. Make a bucket brigade to that pit."

"They must have called the firemen, Sal," Linda panted as she ran. "Sit down and rest your foot a minute. I'll get us pails."

She hurried through the house to the kitchen to grab a couple of kettles and flew out the back door. Ahead of her on the path to the springhouse, Dr. Sutton was struggling with a bulky package, and Linda smiled a little. Apparently, the doctor was taking no chances on damage to his new Orrin Wood. Then she and Sal were running after the others down to the shore.

Below the rubbish pit, men and women alike were concentrating silently on getting water containers to the end of their bucket line without the loss of a single drop more than they could help. But it was a slow, heartbreaking job. Beyond them, the flames leaped, crackling in the dry branches of the pines, and sparks flew ominously, scattering before the wind. Still they fought grimly, passing full buckets and pans up one line, sending empty ones down another back to the beach. Linda worked automatically with the rest, passing, passing, passing, in an endless chain. Behind her, she could hear the rhythmic chop of Steve's ax—and she dared not take a second to look around. Please don't let him get burned, she thought over and over; please don't let him get burned.

125

Then her ears caught the shrill scream of a siren, and a dozen men dropped buckets to spring forward as the pumper tore out on the Head. Volunteer firemen themselves, they went efficiently to work laying salt-water lines down to the Bay while the pumper's crew, volunteers, too, sent the first streams from their storage tank hissing into the flames. Linda pushed her hair away from her hot face and looked back. Steve was all right. He and Waity had chopped their trees down, and the fire seemed to be balked at the trench. Now, with a whole bay full of water to pump from, the fire fighters did not have much to worry about. Sparks still persisted in igniting dry grass, but two or three men with brooms promptly beat them out.

Moving hastily out of the range of the black smoke billowing eastward, Linda glanced toward the house. Dr. Sutton's fresh white paint would be a nice mess. Still, in view of what might have happened, she imagined a little grimy paint would seem a small problem to handle. The doctor went by, hurrying after one of the firemen, and she chuckled at the contrast he presented to his usual immaculate figure. But smoke-begrimed and wet as he was, he looked happy. Linda didn't blame him; the danger was over. She smiled to herself, suddenly remembering her last glimpse of him on the springhouse path. She mustn't forget to tell Mr. Wood how thoroughly its new owner appreciated his water color of Graveyard Head.

17 · The Package In The Springhouse

HEY, Linda! Where the dickens are you? It was Steve's voice, and Linda turned to scan the people drifting toward the back porch where the *Delight's* cook was cheerfully beating on a dishpan and proclaiming gallons of hot coffee. Steve was not in the crowd, but she finally found him down by the rubbish pit, collecting the axes and shovels and brooms that belonged on the Head.

"Would you help me scout around for this stuff?" he asked. "Wait and Bart are still on the fire hose, and I chased Dave and Bill back to help with that mob scene at the house."

Linda nodded good-naturedly. "We'd better prowl around the beach, too," she suggested. "People probably put their pitchers and saucepans down on the rocks after the pumper got here. I know I did. My kettle will be there."

They separated and began to hunt, picking their way cautiously over the soggy ground. Firemen were still on hand pumping a stream of salt water into the thick carpet of pine needles in case the fire had gone under ground, but the Head looked nearly deserted after the throngs who had been in evidence only a few minutes ago. And even the pumper had packed up and left before Steve and Linda had finished gathering scattered utensils.

"Anything we've missed can stay here for all I care," Steve admitted. "If you want to park a minute, Linda, I'll cart the axes up and see if I can find a wheelbarrow in the barn. That'd be the easiest way to lug this junk."

Linda smiled wearily. "You'd better plan on lugging this piece of junk, too," she warned him. "My feet are about to drop off."

But she managed to help load the wheelbarrow and carry an overflow of pitchers when Steve came trundling back. "Let's leave the stuff in the barn," she suggested. "There's enough to clean up in the house now after the party. Then we can just sit tight in the Jeepster and refuse to budge till somebody drives us home!"

Steve wheeled their load into a corner and wiped his smoke-stained face on his torn shirt sleeve. "I'm hungry as a horse," he said as he opened the Jeepster's door with a flourish. "Here, lady, take the weight off your feet. I'm going foraging for doughnuts."

He came back with them, too, plus a boxful of sandwiches and half a dozen brownies, and the pair of them settled down to enjoy life, their legs propped inelegantly over the back of the front seat. Linda looked at Steve's scorched trousers and the runs in her own stockings, and shook her head.

"This has been the dizziest day yet—not that the whole summer hasn't been dizzy enough," she added reflectively, "beginning from the first afternoon when I met you."

"Just consider me on my feet, bowing," Steve retorted, and Linda grinned.

"You know perfectly well what I mean," she said,

128

unruffled. "But today! All morning I could see the crew of the *Yakatak* practically breathing down Dr. Sutton's neck, and by the time we got over here I half expected to find him in irons. And then what happens? Nothing but a nice, normal fire! Oh Steve, maybe we're crazy; maybe nothing is going to happen at all."

Steve swung his feet down on the car floor and shoved himself up. "Well, nothing's likely to happen tonight anyway, and that 'nice, normal fire' you're so pleased with has given me the heck of a thirst."

"I'm thirsty, too," Linda said as she pulled her own feet down and scrambled out of the Jeepster, "but don't let's go to the house; let's go down to the Witch Spring. The water's colder there."

They crunched along the path together, not saying much, just feeling comfortably relaxed, and Steve pushed the door of the springhouse open, fumbling for the light switch that Dr. Sutton had had installed.

"Pure swank," he said, chuckling. "I hope Loraney knows he's done her proud."

He found the dipper and filled a tall glass for Linda before he settled to his own avowed intention of drinking the Witch dry. His thirst quenched, he pulled out his handkerchief to use as a towel and began to splash the cold water over his head and face.

"Oh Steve, be careful. The picture!" Linda's voice rose in consternation. "Dr. Sutton will never forgive you if you damage his Orrin Wood. It's the only thing he bothered to rescue at all."

She pointed over his shoulder at large squarish package wrapped in a patchwork quilt.

"My goodness, it's right behind you. Come over here if you want to splash!"

Obediently Steve moved around the spring. "I didn't even see the doggone thing," he said. "What a crazy place to put it, anyhow. At least, he found the dampest spot he could."

Linda looked worried. "I don't believe we ought to leave it," she told him. "I know Dr. Sutton won't forget it, but it's not even tightly framed, just mounted and stuck in for the show. Water could wreck it if somebody comes in here before he has a chance to stop and pick it up."

"Okay, we'll take it along with us," Steve said. "He'll probably be glad to have it safely back at the house. Wait till I dry my hands and I'll get it."

He skirted the spring again and picked up the picture. "It's heavy enough," he said in surprise. "What do they put on water colors? Plate glass? We can't carry it this way, anyhow, Linda. These cords are ready to drop off."

Linda watched apprehensively as he carried the package across to the light by the door. "Look out, Steve. Don't trip. One of those strings is trailing."

Steve set the picture down as fast as he could and stooped hastily for the cord. "Oops," he muttered in disgust. "There goes the quilt now!" Then, behind him, he heard Linda give a strangled cry and looked up in bewilderment. The picture he was staring at was not Orrin Wood's "Graveyard Head." It was the fresco that he had seen reproduced on the front page of the Portland paper, the fabulous treasure from Pompeii, and leaning against it, partly unrolled, was the slashed-out canvas of Murillo's "Olive Pickers."

Steve hated to look up at Linda. There was nothing either of them could do to help Dr. Sutton now. "This tears it wide open," he said, and his voice sounded harsh even to his own ears. "We've got to get to the *Yakatak*. But what'll we do with this thing?" He touched the fresco gingerly. "We can't take a chance on lugging it all that distance. Anyway, it's too heavy, but you're not staying here without me. Wiggins is too handy with a knife." Steve's face grew grimmer as he remembered the scene on Pinkham's Beach.

"I'll go see if I can find Mr. Wood," Linda said dully. "He might still be at the house." Her face was white and wretched. "Wait here, Steve. I'll be back as fast as I can."

She slipped out the door, and Steve turned hastily back to the paintings. It would be an even worse mess if Dr. Sutton or anyone else barged in and caught him with that fresco. He spread the quilt out as best he could in the cramped space, and laid the stolen paintings on it, wrapping both extra lengths over the face of the fresco for protection. Then he tackled the cord. He had just tied the final knot when he heard footsteps. His heart hammering, he thrust the quilt-covered package into the shadows and jumped across to the spring. By the time the door opened he was casually filling a cup with water.

It was Linda coming back, but Dr. Sutton was close behind her. Relief flared in her eyes as she discovered the quilted package back in place, and Steve tried to smile reassuringly. "Hi," he managed.

Dr. Sutton nodded at him. "Linda thought we'd find you here," he said. "I've just learned you've been on the job retrieving my belongings. Linda says you've been sitting in the Jeepster eating sandwiches, but I want you both to come up to the house for a decent meal. Jack's still in the kitchen."

He moved purposefully around the spring, smiling at them. "I was afraid the fire might damage my painting,"

131

he confessed. "This was the safest spot I could think of on the spur of the moment." Leaning down, he lifted the package awkwardly and turned back.

Steve forced himself to move. "Here, let me help you, Doctor." He had no plan, but he felt less desperate when Linda and he had their own hands on those paintings. "Linda and I can carry that up to the house."

Dr. Sutton hesitated almost imperceptibly. Then he smiled. "I'd be delighted if you would," he admitted. "At least, if you'd set it in the living room for me. That'd save me a stop. I have an appointment and I'm behind schedule."

He put out the light in the springhouse and walked along beside them to the front steps. Then he said "good night" and strode off along the road up the Head. Steve and Linda moved up the steps automatically, but the minute the doctor's footsteps died away, Linda stopped.

"We've got to do something quick, Steve," she said tensely. "Mr. Wood's gone home, but Wiggins is here on the Head. I saw him behnd the lilac bushes by the kitchen just before Dr. Sutton found me."

"Turn around and head back toward the springhouse, Linda." Steve's voice was suddenly decisive. "We've got to get in touch with the *Yakatak,* but these paintings aren't safe at the house. I found an old path on the other side of the Head when I was clearing out the graveyard. It comes out near Loraney's marker. She's going to take care of these things for the rest of the night."

Linda nearly dropped her end of the fresco in astonishment, but she followed him obediently back along the way they had come.

"You mean we're going to put them under all those wild things I made you keep for Loraney?" she asked

132

wonderingly. "Oh Steve, that's perfect. Nobody could find them in a thousand years."

"They're not hidden yet," Steve reminded her bluntly. "Watch your step for Pete's sake, Linda. That path's not going to be easy."

In the darkness the footing was treacherous, and, burdened with the paintings, they picked their way bit by bit. Once they froze to shadows at a sound in the bushes, and Steve felt panic rising in him like a tide. He could have shouted with relief when a small animal scuttled out and fled across their feet. "You okay?" he whispered, and Linda's voice came back quietly, "Okay, Steve."

Finally the path sloped slightly upward and they were lifting the fresco and the Murillo over the low stone wall around the burying ground. Steve led the way along a sanded path toward the far corner, and they set the package down against a tree.

"Loraney's headstone's right here somewhere," he muttered. "We'll find it in a minute."

But he was still hunting, feeling carefully for landmarks, when Linda whistled low. "Over here," she said. "I've found the bushes. Bring the quilt, Steve, while I hang on to these vines."

Working carefully together, they laid the paintings on a crumbling brownstone slab behind Loraney Farr's simple marker and let the tangle of juniper and wild grape fall back in place.

"Keep asking Shubael's Witch to cast a strong spell around them,' Linda murmured. "It's just as important as all the favorable winds she ever brewed."

Steve pulled her to her feet again and headed her toward the farther wall. "We'll stay away from the springhouse, Linda. Climb down on the beach and we'll go up the regular path. We've got to find a phone fast." .

18 · *The Game's Afoot*

I SOUND like a freight train," Linda exclaimed in despair as she stumbled on the beach. "These leather soles keep slipping. Please go ahead before anybody hears us."

But Steve refused point-blank. "I haven't got on rubber soles either," he pointed out. "We started for a housewarming. Remember? IF anybody shows up, we're hunting for a couple of pitchers we left after the fire."

He grabbed her arm to steer her past a litter of driftwood, and they plodded on to the path across the Head. It was a relief to get off the beach, of course, but the walking wouldn't be much easier until the path ran clear of bayberry bushes, and they had lights shining from the house to guide them. So far they had met no one, and with a little luck they would get off Graveyard Head unnoticed. Once they reached a house with a phone, Ed Randall would send someone out in a skiff to the *Yakatak,* and their job would be almost done. There would be nothing left except to point out the hiding place of the fresco and the Murillo.

But the time they had already lost was beginning to get on Steve's nerves. He was not blaming either Linda or himself for the delay. They had merely tackled the first job first, and hiding the paintings was more important than contacting the cutter immediately. Just the same, until both of them were in the hands of the Coast Guard, they were not entirely safe—and Steve knew it. He did not dare to try walking any faster. A sprained ankle to cope with would be the last straw. He could only hope that nothing more happened to slow them up.

Linda was peering in the direction of the house. "There doesn't seem to be any excitement," she said, "and there certainly would be if Dr. Sutton knew those things had turned up missing."

Steve twisted his head for a look. "That's a break," he was saying with relief when Linda nudged him into silence. Then he caught the sounds behind them. Someone was scrambling from the beach onto the path. It was a man, of course. Steve could hear him swear violently as he floundered, and he pulled Linda after him off the path into the shelter of the bayberry.

"We'll fade until he gets past," he whispered.

From where they stood, they heard the footsteps start to pad over the stony ground, but the man moved slowly. Rubber soles and no flashlight, Steve decided. He was wrong about the flashlight, though. A brilliant beam from a powerful torch shot along the pathway for a second, but it wobbled crazily as if someone had knocked it.

"Turn off that torch, you fool," a voice growled angrily, and Steve knew that he was wrong about something else.

There were two men, not one, coming toward them on the path. Steve reached out to grip Linda's hand, and they stood there in the darkness waiting, wishing that they did not even have to breathe. If the man in the lead should happen to be Wiggins, it was probably Dr. Sutton behind him. They dare not be caught in the bushes like spies.

But both men passed by. Then the man in the rear fell heavily, and for an agonizing minute Steve thought they were done for. The torch was blazing across the path again. Another swing to the left and it would inevitably pick them up. He freed his hand from Linda's, ready for fast action, but the first man was already jumping for the light. Snarling savagely, he had spun around, striking viciously at his companion.

"I warned you once. Now give me that light."

Steve could feel Linda stiffen suddenly at his side. Just one brief glimpse of a face by flashlight! He had not been sure, but now Linda thought that she recognized him, too.

"Break your own dirty neck, Max, and welcome." The man who had fallen cursed roundly. "I'm taking care of mine."

"The Coast Guard will take care of it for you if you make much more of a donkey of yourself," the other said angrily. "Now get yourself together and head for that graveyard."

Linda's cold fingers brushed nervously against Steve's hand as they listened to the men's footsteps turn to the right across the field. But until the sounds died out, she did not speak, and even then she whispered.

"It was Max Roberts, the man who tried to buy the 'Dead Ship'! He's in this, too, and he must have followed us somehow if they're going to the graveyard." She clutched Steve's arm in frantic appeal. "Please, please, think of something we can do!"

"I'm trying to, Linda." Steve's voice sounded numb. This was the bitterest blow of all. They could give the Coast Guard the names of three men—Wiggins, Sutton, Roberts—but by the time they reached a phone, the men and the paintings would all have vanished. At least, he decided suddenly, *one* of them and the paintings would have vanished. Roberts would look out for his own interests, no matter what happened to his confederates. Now that he knew someone had found the Murillo and the fresco, he would probably lose no time getting them back in his own hands and skipping.

' Steve swung around to face Linda, his apathy gone. "I'm following Max Roberts," he explained quickly. "Maybe we didn't save the paintings, but we're going to know what happens to them next. If the Coast Guard's got another chase ahead of them, they might as well start off after the right man."

"What do you mean 'I'm following Max Roberts'?" Linda asked quietly. "I don't want to be left behind. Please, Steve."

"I'm not leaving you behind!" The fear that shook him when he thought of it made Steve explosive. "With the kind of reptiles crawling around the Head tonight, you're going to be where I can hear you if you yell!"

He calmed down quickly, furious at himself. Linda had been taking it on the chin all night. Of all the fatheaded things to say to her! What was he trying to do? Break *her* nerve because *he* was afraid something would happen to her?

"I'm sorry," he said humbly. "I guess I had the jitters for a minute. I'll just feel better if you hole up in those lilacs this side of the wall, and let me do the scouting. I've got to know you're safe."

"That's all right with me," Linda agreed readily. "Between these shoes and a skirt I'm a total loss anyhow."

They set out hastily across the field. The grass might be scrubby, but it was still grass, and Steve was no longer afraid of twisted ankles. The biggest problem was their

137

own shoes. To their ears, it seemed as if every time they picked up those leather soles and set them down again they made more noise than a steam calliope. Steve couldn't take it any longer.

"It's no go, Linda," he said. "Off they come." He kicked his shoes off and steadied Linda while she stepped out of hers. "Where did they get to?" he asked as he stooped down to feel around. "I'll put 'em inside mine and collect them tomorrow."

"I stuffed them in my pockets," Linda said carelessly. "Come on; let's go."

They were getting closer to the graveyard now, and they moved more and more cautiously, not willing to risk even another whisper. Steve was heading directly for the lilac bushes. If Max Roberts and his companion were still searching for the exact location of the fresco, those lilacs were the place he wanted to be. They were on the wrong side of the wall, but they were close behind Loraney's headstone. With the night as black as pitch, Steve did not expect to see a thing, but when he and Linda dropped to their knees and crawled between the wall and the lilacs, he was beginning to count on hearing plenty.

There were no sounds of a search, however; in fact, for a few minutes there seemed to be no sounds at all. Then, not far to the left, someone shifted his feet as though he was tired of standing still.

"I want a smoke," he said irritably. It was the man who had fallen down.

"No cigarettes!" That was Max Roberts snapping. "Load your pipe if you have to and see that you keep it upside down."

Listening, puzzled, Steve and Linda heard the faint tap of a pipe bowl against a hand and finally the scrape of

138

a match. The fragrance of tobacco drifted past them, and still neither man moved except to change his position or shift his weight. Steve was growing impatient. Touching Linda to warn her, he slid forward on his knees and began to crawl along beside the stone wall, working carefully nearer to the spot where the two men waited.

Linda stood by her agreement. She trailed him only as far as the end of the lilac clumps, but she stared after him wistfully, trying to pierce the blackness. Steve couldn't be more than a few feet beyond her, but for all she could see of him he might be a mile up the road. It was a nightmarish feeling to be isolated in the dark like this. Afraid of making a noise if she got to her feet, she stayed on her knees, listening eagerly for some trace of Steve's progress.

On the other side of the wall, one of the men moved abruptly, and the other made a low-toned comment.

"Shut up!" Roberts's voice was sharp. "I thought I heard something."

"A sachet kitten?" the first jeered. "What's the matter? You getting nerves? We're waiting for something, aren't we?"

Then, in the silence, a stone rolled noisily and crashed to the ground. Linda sprang to her feet in horror. Both men were pounding for the wall, the torch in Roberts's hand whipping a beam of light across Steve's face. Linda heard Roberts's snarl of triumph as he ran. Steve's arm, caught momentarily in the crevice where the rock had slipped, was giving the man the opportunity he wanted. Unmindful of anything else except Steve's danger, Linda flung herself forward. She needed a stick! Roberts was pinning Steve's arm down with his own. Her loaded pockets, swinging wildly, banged against her ribs, and she

139

yanked desperately at a shoe. Then she was catapulting toward the wall, bringing the heel down on Roberts's wrist with every ounce of strength she posessed.

His arm flew up, striking her roughly aside, and Steve, freed, smashed a fist heavily into his nose. "Run, Linda," he panted.

"Oh no, you don't!" The second man spun her roughly around. "Better take it easy, sister, if you don't want to get hurt."

"Take the torch, Joe," Roberts ordered. "Bring her over and turn it on them both."

He pulled a handkerchief out of his pocket and mopped at the blood from his battered nose. But the revolver in his hand did not waver, as the brilliant beam of the torch brought the whole group into sharp focus.

"Why, it's Miss Cobb and her boy friend again. I felt you'd regret that hasty decision; still I hardly expected you at this hour of the night." His voice rasped sarcastically. "Now start talking fast." The hand with the gun lifted a little. "I'll teach the pair of you to pry into my affairs!"

Steve's hands grew clammy at the ugly menace in Roberts's face, and the bitterness of his self-reproach choked him. His clumsiness was responsible for the fix Linda was in. Then something sang past his ear, and the revolver clattered at his feet. He stared incredulously at the short-handled blade buried in Roberts's forearm. Only one man could throw a knife like that! Wiggins had caught up with them.

With an oath, the man Joe reached for his gun, and Steve launched himself forward, striking the torch from his hand. "Down, Linda," he shouted and dived headlong for her knees. The girl toppled sidewise, the wind knocked half out of her, and Steve, twisting like an eel, made a barricade of his body. From behind them, over the stone wall, a sudden splash of lantern light picked up Roberts making a break for safety, his injured arm clutched to his side. A bullet whined over his head and he tried to run, but he swayed drunkenly, pitched forward, and lay still. Joe dropped like a frightened rat behind the shelter of the wall, his eyes watching the shaft of light move inch by inch over Roberts's sprawled body.

Steve's heart was in his throat. Wiggins was no man on whom to play dead-dog tricks. In back of him, Linda moved nervously.

"Shift your head, please, Steve," she begged. "It's awful when you can't see anything!"

He shifted a bit and waited, every muscle tense, as the light searched out the headstones and the sanded paths.

"I'm coming in to get you, Martens." Wiggins's voice was deadly cold, and the crouching man panicked. Springing to his feet, he ran blindly. A bullet spat on the ground at his heels, and the deadly voice went on inexorably. "No use running; the game's up." A second bullet spattered the bushes, and Joe crumpled. All the fight was out of him.

Wiggins stepped from the shadows and climbed the wall, the lantern in his hand playing methodically back and forth between the two fallen men. "The girl's safe enough now, Purchas," he said sharply. "Get up and collect his gun."

19 • Showdown

THE note of authority in Wiggins's voice brought Steve to his feet, but he could almost feel the knife in his own back. Why would Wiggins care whether Linda was safe or not? For a moment, however, Steve had a reprieve. In the blackness beyond the stone wall, footsteps were hurrying down the field, and though the man never took his eyes off the two figures in his lantern light, he had stopped to listen. Then he motioned with his head.

"Everything's under control, I tell you." The weapon in his hand was steady. "Go get that gun. I'll be right behind you."

Steve's eyes narrowed as he started forward. He would do what he was told. Wiggins had the upper hand. Just the same, that gun might come in handy—if only to use as a club. All he asked was break enough to give Linda a chance to run.

But running out on Steve never crossed Linda's mind. Still huddled against the stone wall, she fought back tears and watched Wiggins shepherd him along the path. She didn't know what she could do, but she had to follow. She couldn't lie like a log on the ground and see Steve marched off. And she had to hurry, she thought frantically as she scrambled to her feet. If that was Dr. Sutton coming, he must have discovered that the paintings were missing. Somehow she had to knock that lantern out so she and Steve could hide. Her heart pounding, she raced after Wiggins.

Already, behind her, she could hear someone bursting over the wall, and then Dr. Sutton's voice shouting, "Wiggins!" But the man with the lantern paused just long enough to call, "Patient over here for you, Doctor. Better hurry," and Dr. Sutton started to run again. Linda darted into the shelter of a clump of hydrangea. She had lost her race against time, but if she rushed in unexpectedly on Dr. Sutton's heels, she could snatch his torch and slam that light out of Wiggins's hand. She simply must not be seen.

Flattened behind the bush, she struggled to keep from panting audibly as she waited for the doctor to pass. She knew that somebody was with him. She had heard a second pair of feet. But it didn't matter. Nothing mattered as long as they ran past without seeing her. The beam of the torch was tangling with the lantern light now; they must be practically beside her hiding place. Then Dr. Sutton hurried by. But he was not the one with the torch, and Linda gasped in wild disbelief. The man following Dr. Sutton was Orrin Wood. Caution gone, she stumbled after him. Questions were making a merry-go-round of her mind, but she held fast to the one important fact: Mr. Wood was standing by Dr. Sutton. No matter how impossible it seemed, Dr. Sutton had to be all right.

Down by Shubael Farr's headstone, Steve had stooped warily for Joe Martens's gun. With reinforcements for Wiggins almost on top of him, his chances of using it were slimmer than ever, but he still had to try. He twisted his head to take a hasty look. Dr. Sutton was just dropping on

143

his knees beside Max Roberts, and Steve, still groping automatically for the gun, shot a glance at the man trying to obey the doctor's orders to hang on to a torch and strip off his coat simultaneously. Wiggins was already forcing the sullen Martens ahead of him, but Steve hardly noticed. He was up and running in the direction of the group around the wounded man. He nearly collided with Linda as he rushed up, and, with her fingers locked in his, they stood together, staring in bewilderment.

Bundled in Dr. Sutton's and Mr. Wood's coats, Roberts lay where he had fallen, the doctor's hands fighting to check the flow of blood from his arm. When Wiggins reached them, Dr. Sutton was busy improvising a tourniquet, and he spoke hurriedly as he worked.

"Loss of blood and shock, but he'll come around, I think." The doctor's voice was grim. "He's got to. Wood and I were trying to find you, Wiggins. I failed to get a message from him early enough tonight, and he's made off with the fresco and the Murillo!"

Steve and Linda started forward guiltily, but Wiggins was already speaking.

"I think not," he said calmly. "I admit I can't put my hands on them, but Miss Cobb and young Purchas might help."

Dr. Sutton lifted his head momentarily, frowning. "Steve? Linda?" He sounded as if the strain of the night's events had suddenly affected the other man's mind. "They didn't know it, but they took the paintings back to the house for me. I walked to the door with them. What have they got to do with this situation?"

"Everything," Wiggins said drily.

Steve stared at him across the doctor's bent head. Ap-

144

parently Wiggins was on the level, but he was tired of fencing in the dark with this man.

"How do *you* know?" he asked bluntly. "Where do you fit in all this?"

Wiggins took no offense. He even smiled a little as he turned to Orrin Wood. "Maybe you'd better explain," he said. "It's going to take time to make my peace with Linda Cobb and Steve Purchas."

"It's all right, Steve," Mr. Wood said quietly. "I just found out tonight. Wiggins's business is knowing things. He's from the FBI. And if you and Linda know what happened to that fresco, put us out of our misery at once."

But Dr. Sutton shook his head. "So long as it's safe, that's enough," he said firmly. "This man needs to get to a hospital. The explanation can wait. Linda can show you where the fresco is, Orrin. I'll need Steve myself."

One hand dropped back on Roberts's pulse, and Steve stood silently at his side. Linda was leading Mr. Wood toward Loraney's headstone, the artist's face a study in astonishment, but Wiggins, with Martens handcuffed to his wrist, stayed close to his other prisoner. Satisfied for the moment with his patient's condition, Dr. Sutton took time to give Steve instructions for getting in touch with the *Yakatak* and bringing back a stretcher detail and surgical dressings.

"The cutter should be off the Head picking up Roberts's tuna-rigged cruiser," he explained. "I got word to her when I found that the paintings were gone. Roberts's skiff must be on the shore somewhere. You can row out in that."

Dr. Sutton evidently wanted that stretcher detail in a hurry, and Steve got aboard the *Yakatak* as promptly as he could. The sight of his brother Bob in command of the captured *Shark* gave him a bang, but nothing could make him want to loiter. The sooner the whole business was over, the sooner he would get an answer to a few questions. He surrendered the skiff to the *Yakatak* and climbed into a tender with the coastguardmen to ride impatiently back to shore.

After that, things moved fast. On the cutter, Joe Martens joined a third prisoner, taken with the *Shark,* and Dr. Sutton saw his patient, safely berthed, headed for hospital care. Last to board were the fresco and the Murillo, still wrapped in the patchwork quilt.

"Wiggins stopped for a look at the *Shark* before she leaves," the doctor said as they watched the lights of the *Yakatak* move down the Bay. "He'll be along shortly, but I vote we wait for him where there are four comfortable chairs!"

Back at the house, Steve stirred up the fire on the living-room hearth and settled Linda in a corner of the couch. She was too keyed up to know that she was tired, and he dropped down beside her to see that she stayed still, anchoring her hand firmly with his own. Dr. Sutton and Mr. Wood went foraging in the kitchen and came back with sandwiches and Cokes.

"First peace of mind I've had in this house for nearly twenty-four hours," the doctor remarked as he pulled his chair closer to the fire. "I never expected to be so glad to get rid of good paintings in my life!"

"It's the first peace of mind we've had ourselves," Linda said, "and if I never see even a copy of a fresco again, it'll be too soon."

Orrin Wood smiled at her. "Confession is good for the soul," he suggested. "I haven't asked any questions, but

146

I'd still like to know how and why those paintings got into that graveyard tonight."

Linda looked hopefully at Steve, and he tried to smile. Explaining to Dr. Sutton's face that you'd thought he was buying stolen goods was likely to be embarrassing. For the life of him, he couldn't think of any tactful way to begin.

"I guess you'd call it a combination of circumstances," he said hesitantly.

"Was I one of them?" Wiggins asked as he strode in and overheard the last couple of remarks. Putting a square flat parcel down on a table, he looked questioningly at the two on the couch.

"You were most of them," Steve admitted. "I heard you talking to Dr. Sutton about muffed chances and contacts right after the second lobster-thief alarm, and the longer you hung around, the more 'funny business' went on."

Dr. Sutton was listening in dismay. "You mean the pair of you have had me on your conscience all that time?" he demanded.

Linda nodded. "But we didn't blame you," she explained. "We tried hard enough, but we couldn't figure out what was going on. We thought Mr. Wiggins was blackmailing you somehow. Even after the *Yakatak* came in, we still blamed him." She lifted her chin defiantly at the FBI man. "You certainly didn't give us the slightest reason to trust you."

"A sketch pad was the most natural excuse for patrolling the shore," he told her. "But you kept turning up wherever I went, and I had to keep you at arm's length I didn't want company. Anyway, I'm a pretty feeble excuse as an artist, and there was no use in calling your attention to it."

"Of course, she kept turning up; we hated to let you

out of our sight," Steve said. Briefly, he outlined the reasoning that had motivated their actions, ending with their discovery of the fresco and the Murillo in the spring-house. "Dr. Sutton played right into our hands. Maybe we were crazy, but keeping the paintings safe looked more important to us than notifying the Coast Guard. Anyway, it's my fault. I suggested hiding them behind Loraney's marker."

"Fault?" Dr. Sutton exclaimed in astonishment. "Great Scott, Steve, if you hadn't headed for that graveyard, Wiggins wouldn't have picked up Roberts and Martens tonight."

"You've lost me," Steve said frankly. "As far as I can see, Linda and I just barked up the wrong tree."

"But you treed the right men," Mr. Wiggins said with satisfaction. "Roberts wasn't scheduled to show up tonight, Steve. He delivered the paintings about two o'clock this morning, and I kept my hands off. We weren't risking the safety of those things in a raid. But the pay-off date was due to be different, and our trap was laid for that." He shook his head. "Roberts just came apart at the seams. He was afraid to wait. Of course, I was here in case of accidents, but between the fire and the party, we failed to find the new instructions from the *Shark*. It was you two I trailed to the graveyard, not Roberts and Martens. I discovered you in a huddle behind the bushes off the path, and why you were still hanging around puzzled me."

"But how did Mr. Wood get involved?" Linda demanded. "I looked for him after we found the package in the springhouse, and he'd left."

"Any resemblance between me and the FBI is purely coincidental," the artist said hastily. "I forgot my coat after the fire and came back for it about the time Dr.

148

Sutton found Roberts's message. Then he discovered the paintings were gone and pressed me into service. We thought Roberts had grown suspicious, waiting, and had made off with them. When we hared off for that graveyard, we were hunting for Wiggins. We were sure the *Shark* and its cargo had slipped through his fingers."

"It's a good thing you did," Linda said. "Until I saw you, I was all set to try knocking the lantern out of Mr. Wiggins's hand, and Steve says he was planning to use Joe Martens's gun on his skull. Roberts and Martens would have loved it."

Mr. Wiggins reached over to the table and picked up the parcel he had put down.

"I was forgetting that I found something on the *Shark* that belongs to you," he told her. "Treat it with respect, young lady. It clinched my first hunch that Roberts was our man."

He held up Linda's water color of the "Dead Ship" for them all to see. "Even if he had bolted without ever seeing Dr. Sutton, we'd have known we were after his tuna-rigged cruiser."

Linda stared at her picture in bewilderment. "But how did it get on the *Shark?*" she asked. "We thought Mr. Rienet had it. And how on earth did it help you?"

"According to Martens, Roberts stole it this morning when people were milling around getting their entries. About your other question," Mr. Wiggins sounded amused, "I overheard a slight argument at the art show. I'd had my eye on the *Shark*, along with others, of course, and from Steve's remarks I gathered Roberts wanted this picture badly. After you moved on, I studied it for a while." He leaned down and pointed out the patched plank on the "Dead Ship's" hull. "The duplicate of that is on the *Shark's* port side."

Linda's face was a fine mixture of emotions. "There goes my artistic ego crawling through a keyhole," she said ruefully, "and I can't even take credit for consciously remembering that patch! I just painted it in because somehow it seemed to belong there."

Mr. Wiggins studied the "Dead Ship" again for a minute. "I'll admit I'm no judge," he said, "but that looks like a pretty good picture to me. Your artistic ego can back out of that keyhole in my opinion."

"Of course, it's a good picture," Steve said impatiently. "Trying to buy it was the most intelligent thing Roberts did. But if the *Shark* was the 'Dead Ship,' why in blazes was she running through the fog that way without a horn? What were they trying to do? Sink their cargo?"

"That was their third misstep," the FBI man told him. "They were posing as tuna enthusiasts, don't forget, and they'd been doing some fishing when they lost their bearings in that fog." Mr. Wiggins shrugged. "Roberts wasn't up to this kind of deal. He was merely a petty thief. Then he got big-time notions. He wasn't smart enough to play a bold game. When the Coast Guard got under his skin, he reverted to type and started slinking. Of course, he nearly rammed you and stirred up more attention."

"What were his other two mistakes?" Linda asked, curious.

"The first was trying to contact a collector named Sutton," Mr. Wiggins said promptly, "and the second was running foul of you and Steve. Actually, the *Delight* had moved to Harpswell Harbor when Roberts was looking for her in Purchas Basin, but he'd just arrived, and wharf gossip indicated she was laid up in the yard. You two raised the lobster hubbub, and he started losing his nerve."

Steve snapped his fingers. "So that's why the *Shark* anchored off the Town Landing that night," he exclaimed. "I remember wondering why a tuna-rigged job hadn't headed straight for Orr's." He grinned at Linda. "I'd make a heck of a Sherlock Holmes. Remind me not to set up as a private eye, will you?"

Dr. Sutton chuckled. "I've had my fill of the role, too," he agreed. "Between Wiggins and Roberts, this has been a fine 'restful' summer!" He glanced with concern at the clock and nodded briskly at Linda. "We're taking you home, young woman," he said. "You've got smudges under your eyes now."

"Please—not till somebody answers one more question," she protested. "I'd never sleep till I got the Tory straightened out. Was he Roberts or Mr. Wiggins?"

The doctor looked thoroughly disgusted. "Roberts," he said. "I was on my way to meet him when I heard that outboard off the wharf and recognized Steve's shout. The man was next to impossible to deal with once he got the wind up. I'd come all the way from Florida and I couldn't get as much as a glimpse of him. In fact, I didn't even know who he was."

Linda was puzzled. "I don't get it," she exclaimed. "I can see that Harpswell Harbor would give him the jitters. Captain Pel told us that even Prohibition rumrunners thought the place was poison. But he could talk to you even if he couldn't deliver the fresco, couldn't he?"

"Not Roberts," Dr. Sutton told her. "You saw the Coast Guard hail him as he came in that Sunday. He didn't trust me or my anchorage long. If he had to clear out without realizing on his little investment, he was not

151

planning to be identifiable. Oh, of course, he made a couple of attempts at personal contacts early in the game, but he fell foul of you and Captain Stover. After that, I could take it or leave it. He was playing safe. Harpswell Harbor was too populous for him, and lobstermen or their dogs were on the shore."

"But what did you do?" Linda asked.

"I took it," Dr. Sutton said. "We had to get those paintings, and Roberts wasn't meeting me in any spot where there might be lights. It was the news in the paper, and the cutter, that finally forced his hand. His cargo was getting too hot, and he had to get it off the *Shark* in a hurry. Your 'Dead Ship' had him worried."

"What a help we turned out to be with that outboard!" Steve said, and the doctor laughed.

"I wouldn't let that prey on my mind," he said cheerfully. "As a matter of fact, you threw another scare into him, and every scare meant another blunder on his part. He merely wanted to settle terms, anyway. He wasn't ready to hand over the fresco."

"But I can see why you were waiting for us on Juniper Point when we got back," Steve admitted.

"I thought you might have glimpsed his face," Dr. Sutton said, nodding. "And you might have spotted my skiff, for all I knew. You both were so obviously bothered by Wiggins, I was afraid you might grow suspicious of me, too."

Linda smiled at him. "Waity tied you in with the performance next morning," she confessed. "He told us he'd seen your Jeepster parked on the Ridge. But we never really gave you up till tonight. All day we kept hoping. Steve said nobody could make him believe you were mixed up in a thing like this of your own accord."

152

"Thank you, my dear." The doctor's voice was affectionate. "Now wrap a blanket around her, Steve, while I go get the Jeepster."

20 · Eight O'clock And All's Well

DR. SUTTON had said that it would take more than Wiggins's new antiseptic reputation to square either of them with Mrs. Purchas when she caught sight of Steve and Linda—and he was right. It took apologies and the whole story of the fresco and the Murillo. Captain Pel and Dr. Cobb sat in on the tale, too, and the three of them asked questions for the better part of an hour. Steve propped Linda's "Dead Ship" on a chair and pointed out the patched planking that had sent Roberts into a tail spin and given the FBI man his first concrete evidence against the *Shark*.

"That picture played a stellar role in the performance," he explained, "and you can give Linda all the credit. She earned it."

"Of course, you didn't put the 'Dead Ship' idea in my head, did you?" Linda retorted.

She glanced around at the others, frowning thoughtfully. "Steve tied Mr. Wiggins in with the 'Dead Ship' almost from the beginning, even when we couldn't make any sense out of it. Sometimes I began to think we were crazy. Nobody else thought he was phony. People just decided he was disagreeable and gave him the wide berth he wanted."

153

"Nobody else heard him talking to Dr. Sutton outside the Grange either," Steve said candidly. "That's what got me. But what happened after we met Mr. Wiggins doesn't bother me much, even if we were off the track. The 'Dead Ship' and that business on the Head tonight worked out all right. It's the lobster-thief alarm I raised that sticks in my craw. If I hadn't butted in then, all this would have been over weeks ago."

Mr. Wiggins looked across at him, surprised. "I guess I'd better amplify a comment I made on the Head," he said. "I thought you understood that one of Roberts's missteps was running foul of you two, but apparently you don't realize what you did that Sunday."

"I realize I scared Roberts out of contacting Dr. Sutton," Steve said disgustedly.

"Fortunately, you did," Mr. Wiggins agreed. "Otherwise, we might have lost him. We weren't sitting here waiting for him, Steve. At that point, Dr. Sutton hadn't even got in touch with us." He smiled at the combination of astonishment and relief on Steve's face. "Stop and think about it a minute. Men like the doctor know they're fair game for half the crackpots and swindlers in the country. He hadn't heard anything about the loss of the Murillo or the fresco; so he simply assumed Roberts's first message was the old forgery racket, and ignored it. For reasons that seemed good to them, the European authorities had refused to let the story break, but the doctor took it for granted that he would have read of a theft as sizable as that from a museum.

Linda eyed Dr. Sutton interestedly. "Then what made you change your mind?" she asked. "Because meeting Roberts was the real reason why you came to Harpswell, wasn't it?"

Dr. Sutton nodded. "At least, it was the deciding factor," he admitted. "I'd been feeling guilty enough about neglecting the old house to play with the idea of a down-East cruise, but I might not have made it this summer if his messages hadn't been so persistent. The man was turning into a confounded nuisance. He'd hinted that he was still somewhere off the New England coast. So I followed his communication instructions and agreed to meet him here. All I had in mind was exposing his swindle."

The doctor's smile was wry. "It was the Tuesday *after* you raised the lobster-thief alarm, Steve, that I finally discovered I was out of my depth. Then I got in touch with the FBI. Wiggins was here before the day was over, thank goodness, for if ever anyone needed professional coaching, I was the man! What I'd have done if you hadn't managed to keep Roberts away from me till Wiggins took over, I still don't know, but I can break out in a cold sweat just thinking about it."

He and Mr. Wiggins rose to leave with the Cobbs, and Steve followed them to the door.

"At least, I feel better," he said, "even if the whole business was pure luck."

But the FBI man shook his head again. "It wasn't luck that frightened Roberts off," he said drily. "You and Linda acted with dispatch. You needn't lie awake tonight blushing for the job you did."

Bob turned up at noon the next day with the news of Roberts's improved condition and the account of the first stretch of the paintings' long voyage home. "They're already on their way to New York," he told them. "There's still some red tape to cut, but they'll soon be shipped out.

Everyone's anxious to get rid of them before anything more happens."

The *Yakatak* was scheduled to leave Casco Bay on Monday, and Bob had wangled a six-hour leave. He spent part of it chasing up his friend Seth Green and the rest of it on Juniper Point, eating his mother out of doughnuts, chinning with his father in the boat yard, and inspecting the partially completed lab for the first time with Steve and Dr. Cobb.

"Why the clams?" he asked curiously when he came across the quahogs in the temporary workshop. But before Dr. Cobb could answer, he was called to the phone.

"They're Steve's charges anyway," he told Bob as he left. "He can tell you as much about them as I could."

Steve took over after that, and the brothers wandered around together. Bob watched and listened interestedly as Steve checked water temperatures, explaining what Dr. Cobb was trying to accomplish for the shellfish industry and for the diggers. "This lab's going to mean a lot to the whole area, Bob. It's the best thing that's happened around here in years."

Studying his younger brother's absorbed face, Bob nodded as if he had suddenly made a discovery. "Doggoned if you don't seem to like even work nowadays," he said.

They were full of enthusiasm when they sat down for supper, and their mother watched them contentedly. Tonight she was almost ready to admit that she couldn't find a single flaw in her family even if it had perversely turned out to be all male. She filled their plates with Bob's favorite clam fritters and listened to the talk drifting casually from laboratory to "Dead Ship" to boat yard and back to the laboratory again.

"That's going to be a great setup over there, Dad," Bob said. "Steve's been explaining it to me. I could go for that stuff myself if they'd only build all the labs on cutters!"

"It'd take more than a deck under your feet to make a marine biologist out of you, young man," his father retorted. "The Purchas Yard would go broke paying for the test tubes you ruined."

"There's faith for you," Bob said, laughing. "Go ahead and blight my budding scientific genius. I'll pass my torch to the other great Purchas biologist. Steve's a natural for those test tubes."

Caught off guard by his brother's comment, Steve looked at his father in dismay. This was neither the time nor the way he would have chosen to tackle the subject. But Captain Pel didn't glance at Steve. He was still listening attentively to his other son.

"No fooling, Dad," Bob insisted. "Steve takes to that lab like a clam to high water. Dr. Cobb says he's already asked for a job next year." He winked cheerfully at his younger brother. "Take another look at him, Captain and Mrs. Purchas. I've finally found out what he's good for. What a relief!"

Their mother's laughing eyes caught her husband's glance a second, and Captain Pel chuckled.

"Boys aren't what they used to be in my day, Deborah," he said, his own eyes twinkling. "Can't tell which way the needle's pointing on their own compass anymore."

He smiled down at Steve's startled face as he got to his feet. "Your mother and I have been waiting for you to get your bearings, son," he said quietly. "A man ought to follow his bent when he has one, and we know there's still more than one way for a Purchas to like salt water.

He held out his hand and Steve wrung it. He couldn't find words at the moment, but his father didn't seem to mind. He pulled out his watch and checked it against the big clock in the corner.

"We'd better be getting Bob back to the *Yakatak*," he told his wife. "Just stack those dishes, Deborah. Steve's going to begin practicing for test tubes by washing these supper things now."

Bob whooped with laughter, but Steve only grinned at him. Give him a mountain of dishes and he could juggle them in one hand! He watched the Ford start up the road for Portland and strolled back to the kitchen with his mind so far from dishes that he washed the coffeepot twice. Through the window over the sink he was keeping an alert eye on the Cobbs' house. Mr. Wood had gone in their front door as Bob was leaving, and his car was still parked by the snowball bushes. Steve splashed the dishwater down the drain and headed for the steps where he could watch in comfort.

Beyond the pilings of Purchas Landing the water of the Basin stirred restlessly. It had been another blue-and-gold day, and later the sky would be spattered with stars. Maybe, before he was through, his work would take him far afield, up and down the coast, but it would always bring him back to the sight and the sound and the smell of the Bay. That was the way he wanted it; the Bay was where he belonged. He peered over at the other house, but the car was still parked by the bushes, and he settled back. He could wait, he thought comfortably; there was lots of time. Linda belonged, too. "Almost like a 'native daughter,'" she'd told his mother after the art show. She had fitted into the Point from the beginning. They would have plenty of week ends together this winter. Proms, too. Hers weren't just vacation roots.

His ears tuned for the start of a motor, he jumped off the steps as soon as he heard a car moving, but Linda was already running down the path. She looks the way I feel, he thought, curious—set to paint rainbows.

"Did you see him?" Linda flung the question at him almost before he caught up to her. "Oh, Steve, he came to talk to Dad after supper. I'm going to study all winter with Orrin Wood!"

Steve whistled appreciatively. "Nice going," he exclaimed. "I always knew you'd get the chance someday though, Linda. I thought maybe even next summer."

"Maybe that, too!" she said, her face radiant. "Oh, Steve, I can't believe it!"

They wandered together down the slope to the landing. This summer and next summer and the summers after that, Linda thought—like this one—on the Point with Steve. Off at the end of the cove the windows of the boat-shop were afire in the setting sun, and she tried to picture Steve at work there with Waity and Captain Pel. She couldn't do it. He belonged in the wing of the building under the pines with his clams and his seaweed and the smell of formaldehyde. Somehow, they must clear the way for him, too. She looked up, smiling, and found him watching her. He had followed the direction of her glance and guessed what she was thinking.

"It's all right, Linda," he said. "It's biology, not boats from now on." His voice was deep with content. "It's Bob's doing. He charged right in at supper, and Dad's with me all the way!"

Linda's dimples were dancing and her face glowed. "A lab's the place I can picture you," she told him, "a lab and a rocky shore. Marine biology's perfect, Steve. For you it's absolutely right."

Leaning down, Steve tilted her chin up until her face was close to his. "You just keep thinking of all the coast-line scenery you could get to paint," he said persuasively. "Then maybe someday I can sell you permanently on a biologist."

But Linda shook her head. "You couldn't possibly sell me, Steve," she whispered. "Because I'm already sold."

Her eyes were soft, and Steve's arms reached out eagerly to draw her close for his kiss. "Don't move now to look," he warned her, "but there's a redheaded man in your life from here on in!"

THE END